# DELE'S CHILD

O. R. Dathorne

# DELE'S CHILD

a novel

O. R. Dathorne

3CP

**Three Continents Press**
Washington, D.C.

Three Continents Press
1636 Connecticut Avenue N.W.
Washington, D.C.  20009

3CP

ISBN: 0-89410-421-7 (cloth)
      0-89410-422-5 (paper)
LC No.: 84-51445

Typeset in Times Roman by A to Z Typesetting
Printed in the United States of America

# Table of Contents

For Hilde, Cecily and Xander Dathorne, my first readers.
For Ernesto Pichardo, my santéro and friend.
For Grandfather, my parents and Esme.
For Marlene Leroy and the late Frantz Leroy.

# PART I

*'Anguish of life, anguish of life' sounds the drum*
*The drum only sounds for anguish of life.*

**Ewe Traditional**

*Death then existed not nor life immortal;*
*of neither night nor day was any token.*

**Vedic 'Hymn of Creation'**

*Though Art be strong. Necessity is stronger.*

**Aeschylus: Prometheus Bound**

*Son, now see the souls of those whom anger overcame.*

**Dante: Divine Comedy**

# PRELUDE

The knife glistened; agent of murder and cure. In the center of the circle the boy-priest stood out in white. Near his feet was the slain lamb, its neck at a lopsided angle, its feet irregularly sprawled in a host of directions. His voice rose, distinct and shrill over the night, commanding the circle of worshippers with its faint and yet insistent cry; in another tongue, one of the past and one they had all forgotten or never knew. The women and men in white shuffled round him as if their feet had been chained together. They gave back a low drone to his high and piercing cry. The little girl looked on.

The grass slightly damp from rain or dew had been made almost dry by the steady shuffle of toes, of bare feet doing a dance that was no dance to a tune that had been left behind in a long midnight packed with terror.

> *Every neighbor is my brother, is my sister*
> *Hear oh hear!*
> *Every brother, every sister is my neighbor*
> *Hear oh hear!*

Back to that night on the topsy-turvy sea, with the sounds of the heavy boots of strangers one flight above, and the dingy sky another story up. Snatched as he was suddenly from the village guarded with palm trees and the sound of morning cock-crow, Grandfather coughed. He too sang in his bunk, where urine flowed in straight lines and there was the heavy stale sweat of the sea and the sweet aroma of a hundred bodies. He did not know why he sang; certainly not for gladness, certainly not because he saw some distant star that told him with certainty of a warm manger or swaddling clothes. But he sang and he thought: This song I will bequeath to those who come after, so that they may hear it in their footfalls and the echo of wind as it travels near them, so that in another land, my own and not my own, they may hear this cry and rejoice that the heart remained in a body broken with pain and constrained to a given space.

The circle in white moved round the boy-priest. In his hand the ceremonial dagger, his feet sprawled over the lamb whose eyes were as open as his forelegs which were in the form of a T. "Every neighbor is my brother." He was even more commanding now and, in one swift movement, as the circle of worshippers chanted the refrain, he brought his knife down, silver clean, swift, to the neck of the savior lamb. Its eyes did not close but it was its love and saving grace that poured out first in a small trickle, then a gush of pure redemption on to the half wet grass. The voices were still low, only the sound of this blood, his blood, slowly dripping into a white tureen. Red blood, clear against the enamel of the vessel. Then the boy sang again and the little girl joined in the chorus.

Grandfather's song still. In that first fast night he had known it all and put into it the misery and yearnings of his children's children. Far from where his navel cord lay, he had been re-born on a vessel. He recalled the silver foam at the end of the sea—his beginning—and the men with different voices from another world. He had called to his gods but they did not answer back; he too had had ancestors and he had called on them, near the sand's edge, where the water lay murmuring, as if waiting for some strange baptism.

He understood nothing at first. They brought him up, sky high he thought, and he looked out of his floating house and saw only the green that was not grass, the horizon beyond which no village lay, the hard floor of the upper deck and the clank of chains shuffling in a circle. High up was the tallest pole he had ever seen, but round it no elders gathered, no children rehearsed with laughing syllables the riddles he remembered, no woman stood in the deepening shadows. And he thought of his young youth and the children he would never sire in a serene home near a river and a field of yams. Instead near the tall post, erect against his day, he saw at eye level a man of a different clan fall, blood draining from his throat. But it was sudden and soon the man had been tossed over the walls of this moving village to the enquiring noise of the grey sea below. And then as quick as a stab-wound, Grandfather had known that this was no alien soul and his head formed what his lips had only partly realized— every neighbor is my brother.

The boy-priest, blood-stained in white, had buried the dead sheep. He had whispered to it, with love and a kindness, the girl thought, that bypasses understanding; he had said that this was his blood and all of theirs and the sheep had gone down slowly into the hole. Over it he had poured the red palm-

8

oil and knelt as he placed the white coconut pieces cross-wise over its body. The chanting started up again, almost by itself, sudden, quick, scaring away the silence of the damp night. The worshippers came close to the grave with handfulls of earth, rich earth which was part of their body and which would cover up the living blood below. One after another, as the boy-priest motioned them, they threw in pieces of earth, of rock, sand, grain pebbles and shells from the ocean. Then the womb-like hole was full and the last spades of earth lay on top like ripples through which the red blood foamed.

Then a woman spoke from the center of what had once more become a circle. She was stooped, pointing with erect fingers at everyone and no one. She spoke with Grandfather's voice, in his tongue, with his syllables, gesticulating as he did when his neighbor fell. Her breast was rock hard for no heart beat there. Deep down there was life, a life that had been kept dead for centuries and made to live at the command of the boy-priest. Through her Grandfather spoke: Where do I go? Grandfather had asked. Where will this village take me? Is there another village near the upturned mortar of sky and wave-water? Who are those people there, these people here? The woman who sleeps chained to my ankle and who screams every night in her sleep—is she another life to which I go?

I feel in me the beginning of promises. I am the ancestor now, Grandfather knew. Out of my sperm will come a new breed. I will people another village and tell them of the old ways. I will have children of all complexions and varieties and these children I will hold close to me, for are they too not my neighbors? They will speak a host of tongues and live in villages to which a person may not walk, unless he learns to tread the water as I do now. They will sow but they will not reap, they will be cursed for many generations, but when they seek out my spirit I will come back and, like this day, the third day of my setting out, I will tell them of the new ways of life in this new world they seek. For it was always a part of them. The moving village means that they can never go back, unless they find both me and my afterbirth and bury me near the sound of a small river and a yam garden. These are my cries, Grandfather said, as he moved down, back to the hole below. Call me near the sea any night, my children, when the wind is rough and there are myriads of things that you do not understand. And I will come as I do now and come again as I did then in the hole of the twitching woman my neighbor. The woman in the slave-ship had screamed when I clawed my way over to her; the movement was unsteady but she had grasped me between her twitching legs and sobbed her love, comfort, desire, hate, bitterness on my wooden chest. Do you hear me? *Every neighbor is my brother, is my sister* and the love I have is gentler than the fall of a leaf on a damp grass floor of my village. I have seen the white shadows coming and going and I have known that my life was not to be like others. Not for me the daily tramp to the farm, the circumcision at puberty, the wife who swings her machete gaily at planting time. Not for me the masqueraders, the aging into an elder, a man of wisdom, known in the ways of the village folk, the harvest.

The possessed woman said: I am an adventurer and I have left my mother and my brother's children to find this new thing that is and is still not. Don't only think of me as the passive pawn of history. I too am a player, of the drums that wake you up in the evening and of the new games I will fashion when I arrive. This indeed is me—I will play the fool, play the drums, play the saxophone, play for freedom and even play the conqueror. I am not a *belafong* for some man's hands to caress delicately as he does a woman's thighs. I am the music, the laughter, the tears, the hopes you have and those you do not have; I am everything you dare to do. I will invent, build and destroy. I will create and murder. I am both architect and arsonist, god and devil. I stand at the crossroads. You wish to know which way to go? Ask of me and I will say.

The woman's voice croaked to a halt. The boy-priest was still there in the center, his eyes commanding the bodies of his followers to obey that voice from the past. And they did, for they felt a new excitement in them, a belief in blood seemingly gushing out of their temples. And they linked arms now and let the love of one for another flow back and forth. Their voices were steadier now and it is with a kind of studied calmness that they intoned the words over and over again for the spirit had spoken to every person's heart. Ask of me and I will say—were those not the words they had heard? And they would ask, again and again and again. For in this new found life lay what they had thought had been lost forever but which was always as near to them as their own blood. And when the boy-priest with a single motion of the hand stopped them, suddenly on one syllable, stopped them, the song continued in their beating blood. This the little girl, Dele, had never ever forgotten.

# CHAPTER 1

Stephan's grandfather was the greatest African. He was large and long, a huge male-man with the index finger of his right hand chopped off. He must have been in love like me, twice or thrice; he didn't say.

No beginning and no end and writing words cannot say it all and stories are weak and life is too personal and lively, too deep in the guts to be compressed into twenty-six letters. And if my feet burn and my heart punches my breast, it is because it cannot all be told, because lived experience is everything and words are weak and that moment, that time and those years were everything in a world without end . . .

It was the first warm time of my young days and light used to smell and Chystelle came on lemonade Sundays and we played with Uncle Edward who was a swizzle stick and wooden walls had names. And Grandfather with a missing finger liked belching after soft drinks. And my aunt had teeth that came out nightly and laughed in a jar.

And Sundays smelt and tasted. Starch and wafers. And once I took ice to church in my pocket because it was hot. But it melted. And Christmas came often and my mother said that a fat man came when I was sleeping and left things I did not want. Night was stark and demanding; I preferred day because light is thin-lipped. At night there is the terror over the shoulder and death that aches at the knees.

At night I know best that the dream is slowly going. I still wake with singing, with water-music and the memory of greendawn in a village, and I remember polished wallaba floors and red Lenny from next door and the Indian shopkeeper and the boy Ali. At nights I taste truth which I submerge during the day. They come up in the first watch between sleep and waking. For me as I grow older they are the only ones that matter and they are all the truth of youth, the truth of a time and a country that has passed and a love without end to which I can never go back.

11

It is not easy to begin at the beginning for it came not suddenly but in surprising starts, flashes of insight into things that I experienced. Or perhaps that is how I remember it. Perhaps it never really did happen or if it did there was all that time the awareness, the innocent experience of the first taste of life, something that is forever gone and which it is difficult to set down. All that I can hope to do is to put it down as I think it happened, the relevant and the irrelevant, the real and the unreal, what touched and what only circumvented. It is the whole that adds up to memory or illusion or that other life wherever, out in a curious dreamland, between the forest out of which we hack our way at night and the morning on the shore and the journey in the ferry-boat that takes us nearer cataracts.

But for me the river-bank is very real. The jungle was real too, silent. It never gave us its secrets, exposed its terror out of which I came. In the sun the pebbles shone and the current curved.

It is at night when the feeling is strongest that the will is weakest. I ask myself a thousand questions and can never - not ever - come up with any answer that seems to make sense. The whole point about my life is that it was all so terribly obvious; it had the dimensions of the terribly conventional and of course it is bound to go along a conventional path to a conventional ending. One knew all this with Dele, in the middle of the summer roses in the park, near the tea-stands and the holiday beach afire with posters and swim-suits; one knew too that although the world we moved in was trampled, very spoilt, a little dirty, that there was something special about us - you and me that is.

There is a meaning that is missing when I change pages, I am startled into a kind of harsh recognition of reality and I am truly conscious that I am making the final journey just as my grandfather and the girl did.

Light is thin-lipped, leans and licks at glass windows. Night is stark and demanding. There is the terror over the shoulder but there is also the resurgence of life that springs from above the knees and it is at night that this must be written, because morning murders with reality. I must tell you how it happened, between the heavy jungle and the impatient hoot of a grandfather's ferry-boat.

\*       \*       \*

12

The next morning Grandfather (like me) woke to the flowers. She was at the window, her blue dress against the lighter blue of the sky. Stephan thought to himself: Let me lie still. I shall want to protract this moment. She doesn't know that I am awake and that I can see her breathing, living and looking. She was kneeling on a chair. She must have just got up, because as yet she hadn't combed her hair and she had wound the blue blanket around her. Let me look and love longer, he thought, because it will never be like this again. Let me love the swell of the small of her back, her two heels crossed, the sides of her elbows, and the shawl she threw against the morning. "Come," she called. She didn't turn around.

He pretended to stir. She moved aside a little and he got up. Below them the Valley Gardens opened up and the grass was pea-wet and a drizzle lay over the hedges. The dahlias flourished in one corner and pink, blue and white and green in another. "The Valley Gardens," she prayed.

"Poetic word," Stephan began.

"Don't be foolish," she shouted at him. "For goodness sake can't it just be the Valley Gardens. Do you have to explain!"

"Hey, hey - wait a minute!" he tried to laugh it off. "I was only - "

She looked at him and suddenly what she had said didn't matter anymore. She jumped down, rapidly, impulsively.

"Darling," she said, "We have four days - just four. Already we've spent one - "

"Let's do something today," he suggested. "Different. After all this was the whole point in coming away. The town makes you into a pendulum. Tick. Tock. Tick. Tock." He started to prance round the room on one leg, swaying his body from one side to another. Suddenly she became serious.

"Do you think?" she began.

"Don't be silly," he reproached her. "It's not the first time." She sat down heavily on the bed. They could hear the bath running in the adjoining suite - the old female buttress next door getting ready to be whitewashed.

"That's just it," she replied. "It isn't the first time. We can't go on and on like this. Sooner or later - "

"Now who is being foolish?" he asked. He made a mock bow, changed his mind and knelt at her feet. "I love you. I love you," he said. "It will be all right." She stroked his hair, ran her fingers along the coarse grain of his chin, put his head in her lap. She bent down.

"Today, my knight," she said, "we shall take the waters."

He looked up at her and when she looked at him her eyes were shining wet.

"The Royal Baths, my lady," Stephan said.

He got up quickly, went to the large cumbersome chest of drawers in the hotel room and started searching amongst a heap of paper and underwear. He swore once or twice and then she said, patiently, as if to a child, "You put it under the bed yesterday evening when we got back from the concert." He ferreted it out and he came and sat by her. He started thumbing through the pages.

"Darling?" she asked, gently.

"Hm?" he replied. He was still turning over the pages. She put her right hand over his shoulder and rubbed her mouth on his neck.

"Who was it last night at the door?"

Stephan closed the guide book with a snap. He got up.

"Look, how the hell was I to know? If everytime you hear a knock on the door we are going to go into a cold sweat, we might as well - "

He was going to say "break the whole matter off" or something like that. But he wasn't brave enough and he stopped and, as usual with them when they quarrelled, the words dried up and became unimportant.

"My knight, you were instructing me about the Baths."

He picked up the book again. "Beauty spots," he said. "Too far." He turned back. "Bands, banks - ah here we are Baths, Royal." She settled back and closed her eyes. She liked to hear him read.

"The Baths," he read, "have the reputation of being the finest in the world. They offer a wide variety of different types of treatment, especially suitable for rheumatism." He started to clown again. "Oh, me rheumatic sides! Tick. Tock. Tick. Tock." She laughed lightly. He liked to see her laugh. He put his hand round her shoulders to kiss her.

The past is not just mine, Stephan knew. It has to do with other people, like Grandfather and things. It is things I remember most vividly - my relationship to things - the smell of gas on a fuming afternoon of great ants; walnuts, brown as skulls on Christmas afternoon and the contact of tide-water as it loosed itself against my bowels. The smell of grass - do you know grass-blades an inch from your nose? Ground in your eyes, the smell of dry earth and damp leaves? The feel of sunlight - and the sound - people only talk of the sunlight that they see, but there is the sunlight that one hears on a still small afternoon, as eloquent as silence.

Of course when one recollects one is in fact re-living the time of feel and power; it is a short time in life everlasting and when it ends no one knows - neither Santa Claus nor the tall male men of that other world, nor worst of all one's self. I do not think that this period of apprehension and quake, of waking

14

at night fired with the strings of guitar sound, I do not, I say, think that this period ends abruptly. There is a petering out; and perhaps as one grows older the saddest realization that comes is the one that one can never grow up from maturity.

When a man reaches back and pokes about in the past and tries to piece it all together he has to think in conventions. People will talk, when they do, of their setting out, the initiation into first love and finally of arrivals. But the small girls that two of us remember are the same; the schools and the departure, they are all the same. Because we are all living one human life; the thing that is you and me is only a variation. So let us talk now of variations.

The first is that I don't remember all, Stephan knew. I remember a little and that not well. I cannot be sure how much of what I say is true, but I suppose that it is true in the sense that all things are true. It's true in the sense that even if it did not happen in the way I say it, because I say it now I make it true for now and for all time. And when I talk of school I remember first the Fridays when we made a world from plasticene with clumsy fingers. I remember Louise who taught us two times two are four, three times three are nine. (She eloped afterwards with a dentist - why a dentist? I wonder. Why on earth a dentist?) I remember the old frail matron who kept the school. She belonged to the decaying shreds of Creole upper class. Her husband was a Mr. Something, Something M.A. and my god he never forgot the M.A. He introduced himself as Mr. Something, Something M.A. He was a so-called solid figure in the days of colonial governments and eventually was rewarded with a place in the Legislative Council, an order of the British Empire and a pair of crutches.

In their backyard was a large mango tree. Mangoes are green but the insides are squelchy yellow. They ooze out on the fingers. Mangoes are bright-star bright - and the stalks are the color of sand. In mango-time the mangoes smelt of sugar and tasted of syrup. There never has been a mango-time like this, when the rice balls tickled the thin air and the overripe fell plonk plong and we crushed it and ground it into substance.

Once a boy had beaten me and told me I was stupid. Another time a girl had walked on my feet for a solid fifteen minutes. And how big was everybody then. The boy and girl I know now could not have been more than six or seven but then they seemed tree tall.

We went to Sunday school. At Sunday school Mr. Rogers cracked his thumbs and said that we should repent, believe. At Sunday school there was a tree that grew sky-high, over the altar and through sky-light and painted glass it seemed to me always to have something to do with the flood. In a way it was the

15

first tree that ever waved so high, sky-high, over the harvest of wafer, wine and the cleansed faces of those who were truly innocent. Then we sang revivalist hymns, with rolling choruses. In church there were huge men in the last row, men with voices like bass-drums who refused to sing in tune. They bellowed lustily to God and heaven-high and clapped in double ecstasy for the ends of lines and middle phrases. We were whole and holy in those days and sent huge chunks of song to sky on God Sundays.

On Good Mondays a woman came with the children's washing. She had known better days. There was an elaborate system attached to every house, which consists of what is known as a back step and a front step. It is expected that one's friends, the local clergyman and the postman may come up the front stairs. The back stairs are reserved for newspaper boys, cooks, washerwomen and the vast assortment of people who call at houses in a never ending routine. To break this rule was to bring down recriminations on one's head. The woman who came on Mondays broke it - every Monday. My mother said little - she was tolerant. But the defiant way in which she received the clothes left no doubt that she felt that it was by special license that she allowed it.

Grandfather sat in a rocking chair in the front room, called a gallery, and drank Coca-cola and belched and rocked and drank Coca-cola and belched and rocked. Grandfather had been dead for the past ten years.

At first Grandfather was an infrequent visitor - he had something to do with the ferry boat that chopped a sluggish way up the river and we only saw him when the ferry boat was in for a night or two. He was large and black, his left fourth finger chopped off down to a small independent stump. For children his large face was like a hunting ground - one could chase after the strings of white that had got into his pores and squeeze them out, I remember his head was completely bald - and that is all I remember - the rest is what happened.

And what did happen? Nothing. I came at the tail-end of his love-time; he had acquired two wives, a compound full of children, various women we respectfully addressed as "aunty", a small curly-haired boy from none of them which he and all of us called Salvador and a large dog. When he came to spend the odd nights, he brought the even nights of the darkness up-river with him and the small vivid mystery of wharves growing against jungle. When he shook hands, the stump of his half-finger twitched erratically. He said, "When I die, I will come and haunt you." We believed him as children; and of course he did and does. His ghost grew with me, a large unpleasant type of ghost, that had to be placated with soft drinks and large heavy meals; a demanding ghost that gave violent tugs at me when I insisted on following in Grandfather's footsteps.

16

He was not always somebody's grandfather. He was a boy once. I am almost sure he could have been Stephan.

If there was a beginning it was perhaps fifteen years ago. I am sure that you don't remember Dele - you could not possibly. It was a casual act - we commit a hundred everyday - riding seawards between the jungle and the cataracts - and we leave no mention in our diaries. But it was Sunday afternoon I remember - rainy season. I rode over a puddle and your brother had said something that made me laugh. I looked up. I just remember seeing you - it was not the first time of course. We had played before - that afternoon I knew we could never again. You had become a woman - a beautiful woman with short black hair and large eyes and there was a mystery between us.

It is necessary to get it all clear - that is why I wrote it all down. Do you understand? It is necessary to get it all clear because I must speak the truth about how the ferry-boat crashed on the rocks and how Grandfather coughed his last cough and the undertaker sympathized and that night they sent him on his final journey downstream to the cataracts and his women wept.

Do you love me? I have asked myself that question a thousand times. Before I was brought to prison I used to wonder what it all added up to. Did he love me? Grandfather I mean. He had a broken finger, just the edge of a right finger left, and he drank and belched and rocked fast in a high chair. Did he love me? You would have loved Grandfather. He spent his summers in a spa like you and me. He drove a ferry-boat down-river, avoiding cataracts, where we all go, skimming the edge of jungle, where we all come from.

"Do you love me?" Dele, the girl in jeans asked in the park. The summer was blazing and the sky was ink-blue. "Do you love me?" the girl in jeans asked near the river. We were on a motor-boat and Dele had steered and said she was happy and she had loved the lap of brown water and the brush that grew near the coast. The man had warned us to keep away from the banks.

No beginning and no end and writing words cannot say it all and stories are weak and life is too personal and lively, too deep in the bowels to be compressed into twenty-six letters. And if my feet burn and my heart punches my breast, it is because it cannot all be told, because nowness is everything and words are weak and that moment, that time and those years were nothing in a world with end . . .

*     *     *

17

Grandfather and I must have had the same girl but I cannot be sure, Stephan thought. She lived in a white house in a small village by the sea. She was a small girl, her toes were pointed straight out and she used to wear moccasins, that wrapped them up. I do not think that I ever saw her toes. Her toes were a little curved, a little bent in the open sandals that she wore. She was just a little taller than me and she lived in a grey cottage, at the edge of the savannah land that tipped the coast. My grandfather had married her and they had lived together for years, it seems, in a small yellow house in the busiest street in the town. They said that I was tall for my age and that I should not eat sweets. There were other people - Uncle Edward (a swizzle-stick) and the girl. She had something to do with the swing in the long front room. When she pushed me up I went higher into the clouds. In the ledges of the clouds my father had planted bread that brought mice and kept away poverty.

"Boy," my grandfather had said. The girl was dead and he had retired. "Go an' buy a sweet drink." I ran out of the blue house into the street and towards the dairy. Rampersaud was a thieving man who poured milk in his water. I said that I wanted a drink.

"For you grandaddy?"

Rampersaud pointed to a notice in his shop - Credit makes friends, cash keeps us as enemies.

"He send money?"

Gingerly I took out seven cents. Rampersaud coughed and took each coin, singly, one by one, counting them.

"From now on he have to pay for the bottle. Tell him next time is three cents for the bottle."

He gave me the soft drink and I skated out into the streets. I had always wanted skates like the rich boys who played on the sea-wall on a Sunday. We had nothing - no swing, no skates.

When I came out of the shop with the girl she asked me about the next day. It was the last day of the year. She had come down from the white house by the sea and she was going to stay for the night and we were going to go dancing. That time I was not skating - I was driving a car - a golden one. I used to park it in the sun and walk with the girl.

They said that when my grandfather met the girl she was beautiful. She had long hair, she was dark and tall and she was silent. Her parents had objected.

"Why you want a coal-black man?"

"He is not a coal-black man."

18

"He is a coal-black man."

"These high school girls!" My grandfather drove a ferry-boat up-river, steering past the cataracts and avoiding the swell and push of the water. There were aunties up-river who came to town and once an aunty had come and said, "That Portuguese man is no good."

I had loved him. He was black (I think), and he had been baked into coal by the sun; he had been exposed to the sun in the sail-boat that he drove down river. Once it had crashed. Grandfather had died and the girl had cried eyewater and the aunties had cried and Salvador had come from up-river threatening to sue everybody if he did not get his share. But they were laying down the sewage in the yard at the time and everybody said, "Salvador - you cannot get what you do not want," and Salvador had escaped to another country.

I had first kissed Dele that night when she stayed over for Easter. I had kissed her near the sea - the brown sea that was blown to thread and she had said something about a sail-boat that had been wrecked far out. The girl had said that this was an important moment and that I have lived it with her. When I got home Grandfather had died.

He had died one night riding blindwards on his feather bed, belching hot fumes of cold drink, vomiting his years of sweet drinks gone sour after the burial. I had never really loved him. I had loved the girl but when he died I used to think that he would come back and take me away. I didn't want to go, especially that Easter when the whole world was sweet and beautiful, and we rode and sat on the sand, high above beach water.

Once we had leaned over a bridge and Grandfather had come with his ferryboat, between the rocks. The girl had recognized him and had said, "He is a no-good Indian."

Grandfather had courted the girl after he had returned from active service during one of the world wars. She was a yellow woman and she used to sing in the church choir and Grandfather had come off the steam-ship and had told her tales of his adventures among the rocks and the clean dead and the razor-sharp sea and she saw and said, "But you are a great man. And you are all I have. This is an important moment for me."

He had the first radio on that side of the street. The importance of this cannot be over-emphasized. People used to crowd up his front-stairs shouting, "Just turn it on let we hear chuks, chuks. Just turn it on let it whistle - then we go go."

He was a sea-man and when he went he took a little plug with him so that no one could play the radio till he got back. The girl had liked it. She said to me, "It's a battery radio?" She was walking home after church and I had stopped her on the way. She looked round cautiously.

"I like the radio. But you shouldn't have come. You know Daddy, eh, don't know Daddy? He will be cross. Daddy will be cross."

"I buy it so that we play with it when we go riding."

"You have no bicycle and I am not lending you mine anymore."

"But I am always careful," I said.

"You will mash it up. You drive it like a boat."

"The last time it wasn't my fault when it ran into the rock-wall." She had walked away saying, "Since when bicycle does move by itself?"

I hated her but she was Grandfather's love and I had loved him for one whole boyhood in between his coming in and his lying down. He had hanged himself from the swing in the garden and the girl had bellowed. "Why? Why? Why?" She never was one to say too much. Throughout my childhood all she had said was why, why, why? She hung from the wall in the drawing-room near the swing. That was where I had first kissed the girl. And she had said, "This is not important. I have to pass my examinations. This is not important."

I remember distinctly that it was on that day in the very month of a specific year that I had met the girl. She said, "We related to each other." I have never even kissed her. My grandmother was a photograph. The girl had said, "He is just a ugly Chinese man with a red bottom lip." My grandfather had said nothing. Throughout the years he had said nothing. He only spoke once to Uncle Edward the swizzle-stick and all he had said was why, why, why?

I remonstrated with the girl, but she did not reply - all the years she had just been there with an enigmatic smile on her face and she had said nothing. Red woman, black woman, red man, black man. I never knew them. They had died while hunting in the forests. He was a tall strapping Aboriginal and she was Chinese or something and they had died together singing, locked in one another's arms, one trip above the waterfall.

When I showed Dele the two photographs she had looked and asked me why, why why? This girl was beautiful. She wore low-heeled open shoes and she used to like walking in the cemetery waking the dead. I had kissed her before she died and my grandfather had coughed his sickly cough and laughed. He said, "The boy gro'ing." I did not grow. He was my grandest grandfather and I took my later name - Grandman - from all he was.

# CHAPTER 2

Later Stephan was to think back on the boy's first visit. Every evening after dinner he used to sit out on the verandah. It was murderously hot inside and the ceiling fan just seemed to be churning hot air round in circles. At least he could see them pass by. Just think of me, he used to reflect, a trifle whimsically, not yet thirty and semi-retired. What the hell was he doing in Africa anyway? Build a road they had said and it had sounded interesting, even a little exciting; nine months and he would be out and away. Back to San Francisco and he could spend some hours beguiling his friends on what he had done and where he had been. This one letter would prepare the way. "Tea, Sah?"

It was James, punctual as hell, fresh from his afternoon nap. The sun was beginning its rapid dive behind Mr. Frost's house. He put down his pen and paper. "No James." It was a daily ritual. He added this time though. "Haven't I told you Americans don't drink tea?"

James was not sure whether he should laugh or not.

"Except in a bag," he added. "U'know, with hot water - "

His mind wandered off. Some people had started walking up the hill near Frost's house.

"Who are they James?"

"School children, Sah."

"School children?"

"School children."

After a while you began speaking in monosyllables here. They seemed to say as much as a whole sentence. It was part of the ritual of being here, of being part of an enormous society in which you did not have to make a sound to ensure that you were alive. Perhaps he might even grow to like it. Hopefully he would not end up speaking like this. Back home the consequences would be disastrous! But it was good, for now, to have your words accepted before they were understood.

Goddamn school children, he thought. That's what I'm looking at. Not at a good show, not even an adult peek show in a downtown bookshop in Frisco. Real live school children! For a moment he had forgotten that James was still there, but James had a way of ensuring that he remembered. James would flick something off a chair or move his bare feet, scratching one against the other. When Stephan looked round, he realized that there were two people standing there. He started folding his paper.

"My bruddah, Sah," James stated. The boy was about fifteen, slender, dark, with almost no hair on his head. He came forward, bowed slightly and put out his hand. "How do you do, Mr. Hamilton." Stephan was so startled that he got up and shook his hand. Shit, he thought, must be one of the students. None of the goddamn humility that James always exhibited. "My name is Sarki," the boy remarked, "Sarki Bello." The handshake was warm.

"I'm Stephan - Stephan Hamilton," he tried to smile back. He could smell a crispness on Sarki's clothes. "Have a seat," he stuttered. Sarki moved elegantly into a nearby seat, changed his mind and perched himself on the concrete ledge that ran round the patio. Sarki looked at him as if waiting for him to begin the converation. James had vanished, taking the folded letter which he would seal and post to the States.

Afterwards Stephan was to recollect this meeting and wonder why in hell he was so damn uncomfortable. He felt he knew that answer then, but that was several years after. At that time he remembered looking out again and realizing that the sun had vanished with James, and Mrs. Frost or one of those damnable kids had put on the lights in their house. He preferred the semi-darkness.

"James told me about you," Sarki said.

"Oh?" He reached for a cigarette and Sarki watched as he lit it. Stephan remembered afterwards that he did not see the children go past that evening. Sarki wore open sandals and his toes hung loosely round them. For some reason Stephan kept looking at his toes as he lit a cigarette. Sarki perched at the extreme end of the concrete ledge with his feet straight out. His head was on one side.

"I go to school in town. James tells me you're building the road there."

"Yep. It's a hell of a job. Mosquitos, soft surfaces, my boss," he pointed in Frost's direction, "everything - "

The boy laughed. "What do you do it for?"

A sudden, direct question. He exhaled some smoke but felt that his throat was all clotted up. He got up and turned on the porch-light suddenly, like a guilty man. He tried to laugh it off and switched the conversation.

"Is there much fun here?" Sarki was squatting opposite the chair he had been sitting in and his eyes looked directly at Stephan's.

"Stephan - may I call you Stephan?" he went right on, "You can't find it here for certain, on your patio, looking at the other houses - "

He felt like telling him to go to hell and kicking him out. In this part of the world his three months' experience had taught him this much: young boys do not speak to grown men in this way. But there was something about Sarki that was so damn cocksure, very different.

"I figured I'd do my nine months and split," he heard himself replying. "Why the hell should I bother to get involved with anything I can't finish?"

Sarki nodded his head. "Maybe you're right."

There was silence for a moment. The crickets had started up now, their weird whistles seeming to come from all directions. "Or maybe not."

He stubbed out the cigarette and crossed his legs. He must try and get some control of this situation. After all he worked with men, everyday, grown men, who called him "sah" and who looked up to him. Even Frost couldn't do damn much for sure if he wasn't around. Maybe there was some sense after all in the interview back home. Three white-haired men round an enormous table and he at the other end.

"Do you feel that you can handle this?" from one. He explained, he lied, he invented. He needed it. It was a good thing for he was fairly sure that the company of Davidson and Son (what a ridiculous name) wasn't going to keep him on the payroll indefinitely as their lone black star. For it was as such that he had been hired in the sixties. He had messed around for a while after college, selling insurance, working as a personnel officer, drifting from Charleston to San Francisco, threatening himself that he would go back to college. And then four or five years ago he had seen an advertisement in a California paper and Dele had told him to apply. So he had and - "Sure I can handle the damn job." He thought, "Ain't it niggers you talking 'bout? Niggers is niggers. I've seen them all. Lil itty niggers, big mothers, smart ass yellow ones and funky black ones." Instead he said, "I think I can manage. I feel an affinity with Africa." It sounded well, even elegant.

Interview jive talk. Didn't believe it then nor now. Anyway it landed him the job and a decent salary which meant he could get back next year and shack up with Dele, maybe even get married, have kids, screw like everyone else on Fridays and Saturdays and like all good folk, borrow a great deal, live well, watch a baseball game, keep out of the Mid-West and holiday in Florida with Dele.

"You want a drink?"

Sarki nodded. "Don't tell me it's tea?" from him.

"No," Sarki laughed easily, "something stronger. I'll have a Coke."

"James," he yelled. Soft footfalls as James re-appeared from nowhere. "Get him a Coke," he drained his glass. "I'll have a scotch. Easy on the ice."

He felt on surer footing now. James went in, re-appeared, said did he want anything more as he wanted to leave, disappeared and Sarki announced, "We're related."

Stephan reached for another cigarette, lit it and said, "Yeh. He told me brothers. Or cousins, whichever - "

Sarki gave an impatient twitch. "Not him and me. That's how we speak. Every neighbor is a brother round here. You and me."

Stephan put down the cigarette. Now he thought I'm either going to have to kick his ass out and tell him about his momma or listen to some bullshit for the rest of the night. He decided on the latter. There really wasn't much to do. He didn't feel like reading; the new African literature was driving him nuts; everybody had a book out, full of proverbs and ancestral wisdom and at least one death. He had asked his buddy Pietro to send him some stuff from City Lights but it hadn't come yet. No television in the whole goddamn country. "Sent me out to go crazy! Trust white folks for that. First they take you out of the goddamn place, put a bangle on your ankle, chain up your ass, then they free you, call you a citizen and send you back.

"Let me tell you about me," he interrupted. "I'm a horrible, nasty American. What you folks round here like to call a Yankee. And you know something else? I was born and raised in South Carolina. I live in California now. With a name like Stephan Hamilton, I'd make a fine African boy. And I didn't even change my name so folks could pronounce it. No sir I'm a bona fide U.S. nigger, just like you're a bona fide African nigger."

"Fulani."

"What - oh your tribe, ethnic group, whatever." He could clown his way with this one. He blew two more smoke rings, stubbed out the cigarette and repeated, "Nigger." Sarki looked at Stephan for a few moments as if he thought he had gone mad. Then Sarki said slowly, very slowly, as if to himself, "You and me, we are one." The finality of the statement struck Stephan as a little overdone. Stephan wondered pleasantly to himself why James had taken it upon himself to introduce him to a lunatic.

24

                              *       *       *

He had not yet died and in the compound of the palace the children's voices would be clearly heard. They danced in the sand and sang. They laughed when the clown walked across on his hands making fun of Emir Sarif Badian's stomach. For only he could have dared to do that. The Interpreter walked just a little behind, stone-faced, and the attendants brought up the rear. Emir Sarif's gown was white and it trailed slightly on the dusty floor of the palace as he made his way into the next chamber. He stopped to pat one of the children on the head and, after standing still for a moment, she raced away in some embarrassment.

Emir Sarif made his way to the council chamber. Already some of his clan had gathered and were squatting on the dirt floor. They kissed the ground as this elaborate man made his way up to a dais and sat down drawing his garments closer to him. The Interpreter stood near his left and Queen Abu sat on his right. She was fairer than he was, a young Fulani woman with short tight lips and a beautiful glistening skin. She was as quiet as a stone.

"First," the Interpreter said, "we will acknowledge the princes who have come to the court to pay their obeisance."

Emir Sarif barely inclined his head to one side where, through an open door, just under the trees outside, the princes, some twenty or so, had gathered on horses. The Clown jumped around his feet and began moving like a horse, hitting himself on his own behind. The Emir glanced down, whispered something to him and the Clown then hopped on to the Emir's chair and replied in his ear. Emir Sarif laughed; the Clown hopped down and away. The faithful bowed. For the Clown had received his payment - enough it was for him that Emir Sarif had deigned to laugh. Queen Abu did not move, still as rigid as a statue. A man among the faithful rose and knelt, rose and knelt, a bobbing action which few perceived since they still sat, hands cupped, looking at the sandals of Emir Sarif. When Emir Sarif did acknowledge him, the man's words were addressed, as they customarily were, to the Interpreter, "Shall I saddle the Emir's horse?"

The Emir nodded and the Interpreter answered back. The Keeper of the Stables left suddenly but with a quaint dignity. Soon it was obvious that the lesser princes on their impatient horses had heard that Emir Sarif would come out. The horses pawed impatiently on the ground. The Emir stood and the faithful knelt. Only the sound of rustling silk and the distant voices of children playing could be heard. The Clown was silent in the Emir's seat.

"As you know I go to Mecca for my third pilgrimage. May the blessings of Allah be with you all and may you find peace! Let no man lust after his neighbor's wife! Let no man seek another's goods but always give alms. Remember to acknowledge Allah five times every day and always remember that there is no god but Allah and the Holy Prophet Mohammed is his spokesman."

The Emir walked out slowly, the Clown doing his dance, the Interpreter and the attendants not far behind. When he got out into the sunshine, under the mango tree, where his horse was ready, he ignored the antics of the Clown lying under his horse. After he put his foot on the stirrup and he felt the sturdy, strong frame of the horse under his clothing, he looked opposite to where the princes were, ready to do their charge. They would ride down pell-mell towards him, their horses stirring the ground, reigns slightly loose in their hands, and would stop, abruptly just inches away. His own stallion, proud in its prime, would not budge an inch, nor must it for was he not their lord?

The children had come from the other chamber and were standing outside in the sun. The beggars crawled round on their knees seeking largesse. The princes began their mad race towards Emir Sarif. He looked at them; their slender lean bodies swaying in the hot noonday sun as their horses drove them with suicidal determination towards him. At the back of his mind he thought of the sheep that had been slaughtered for victorious celebrations after their rough charge towards him, a charge that usually left their horses foaming at the mouth and emptied them of their pocket valour. In the chambers later that night they would bring him gifts and kiss his feet as a token of their submission. Then, suddenly, Emir Sarif folded up, tipped over and fell.

No one knew how or why. Queen Abu had remembered gasping back a shrill scream as she saw his body turn over on his horse. The Clown thought he saw Emir Sarif's body tumble off his rearing stallion and plummet on to the ground. The Interpreter recalled something like a wind, a fierce wind, passing by his side as Emir Sarif's body flew down. But Emir Sarif only saw the dust and the horse's hooves and heard the screams of the children, no longer jubilant, as he crashed down to the cardboard earth. Near his mouth was one of the horse's hooves of a lesser prince and he thought that he remembered kissing it before he died.

At least that was the song of his family that the griots sang to the new Emir Muhammed early one morning about five years later. He had inherited his father's pride and his shame as he fell down at the feet of a lesser prince. Emir Mohammed the Wayward, the griots had teased him; perhaps there was a hint

# CHAPTER 3

A crowd waited under the street lamp at the corner. The police noisily redirected the traffic. The loud speakers spat out imprecations; a political meeting was in progress.

"An' is the opposition we thinkin' of," someone was saying.

"After all the Whites can't have everything they own way. They representin' the White people on the island and we is blacker in complexion. No White can represent a Black."

The crowd cheered. Another speaker followed who seasoned his oratory with numerous indecencies like fruitcake. The Blacks were exercising their right of opposition according to the conditions of the British constitution. For the Whites and the Blacks were the two main people of Iota. There were other minor groups but these were too small to be considered. However they included the Light Ones, the Yellow Men and an extremist group who called themselves "people." The latter were thought to be Communist in some circles.

The reason why the Whites were called Whites and the Blacks Blacks was a burning and colorful issue deeply rooted in Iota's re-written history. In the old days Iota was populated by Indians who discovered Columbus. When the slave-trade started, ships on their way to West Africa and the West Indies for their cargo of slaves often called at deserted Iota to leave any of the more infectious cases of illness. These people were left on the shore with bread, water and a hastily administered prayer and then the ship sailed on. An ancient legend says that the first man to land on this island was one Euraf - now a god - who determined to make the island a haven. (The Neo-Iotan historians explain that it is from his name - Eur and Af - that the term Europe and Africa came into being.)

Both the Blacks and the Whites assert that Euraf was neither color but "half and half" which in Iotan means he was neither one nor the other. They claim that both Africans and Europeans on the island are his descendants.

Now the Blacks who occupy the island claim that they are brown brown, that is that their race is untainted and that they are the true inhabitants. They are dark in complexion and the majority of them support the party in opposition - the Brown Party. The Whites on the other hand claim that they are better owing to their complexion (most of their ancestors came to Iota when slavery was abolished). They are fair in complexion and the majority support the Fair Party. There are however some complications worth mentioning.

The first is that not all Black people support the Brown Party and not all White people support the Fair Party. Some interchange parties and some others who have been abroad, believing they were neither Black nor White, were rudely dubbed "niggers." So they came back and called themselves Iotans. They formed the I.I.I. (Iotan Independence Interests) but they are believed to have socialist sympathizers and to be intellectuals, so no one takes them seriously. They have further made themselves unpopular by wearing their shirts out of their trousers, growing beards and having socialist literature sent out airmail to them.

Now the Brown Party was having a political meeting because word had been received of the impending independence. They took their functions as members of the opposition very seriously and assiduously opposed everything the government supported. Consequently independence to them was a very dirty word.

"An' that is what I t'ink 'bout independence," the speaker was saying. He spat liberally, neatly between the shoulders of his supporters. The meeting shouted. The speaker continued:

"Anyhow I ain't sayin' nothin' more. I leavin' the rest to our leader and Prime Minister in Opposition - Rev. Two-for-Three.

The crowd broke into loud applause. A fight started at the back between a White and a Black but the traffic police soon ended that by beating both parties with a truncheon. Rev. Two-for-Three came forward smiling. He raised his right hand and gave a blessing to the people. They all said "Alleluia" and the Rev. Two-for-Three smiled all round. He had been given that name in the old pre-ordination days when he used to go from house to house buying bottles at two for three cents. When he had collected enough bottles (and money) he had founded a church called the Iotan Epistolic Church and ordained himself. He had also formed a school where he taught grammar and this had left him with an incurable habit of punctuating his speeches. From here, in a religious-conscious community, it was not difficult to become the "Prime Minister in Opposition."

"Eh! Eh!" Rev. Two-for-Three began. "But is what I hearin' at all eh (Question mark). People whisperin' (Bz, bz, bz) all over that independence comin' like a train (Chuk - chuk - chuk)."

As he spoke the crowd cheered. They liked his oratory, for in addition to punctuating his sentences for them, he gave onomatopoeic sounds to accompany his statements. A student at the back shouted, "Who gave you the right to turn round your collar?" Two-for-Three ignored this and continued:

"But are we ready (Dash) is this place ready (Question mark). I ask what shall I do? He questioned the people on the west side of him and they said, "Join the Fair Party." He laughed a bitter laugh and asked some people on the north. They replied, "Form another Party." Then he turned to some people on the east and they replied, "Have a party."

Rev. Two-for-Three can be forgiven for losing control of himself.

"You silly bastards," he shouted. "At this time you tellin' me jokes eh (Question mark). You people on the east should be wise but you are damn fools (Period)."

He addressed the crowd to the South of him:

"This independence business is doin' no good for we Blacks (Period). No good (Period). We must stop it (Comma, I mean period). So tonight we gwine visit Paradise and mek trouble. The world will see Iota is not ready to govern itself. England let we down with this independence business. Is an imperialist plot (Period, close inverted commas)."

*     *     *

The Prime Minister, Sir Ianty Pakeman, was trying on a new suit. The tailor kept making calculations with a pencil in his mouth. At the same time the P.M. was holding an important cabinet meeting a few hours before going to the Paradise Hotel.

The Minister of Health coughed and spat. He had a permanent cold.

"We must talk about this Brown Party threat," he bellowed. A portable radio played American pop music.

"It is not your affair," the Minister for Internal Affairs said sourly. He was designing a special Cadillac for himself on his pad and considered the entire meeting a waste of time.

"Not yet," the P.M. ordered. "Let us hear from the Interpreter what actually has happened."

The Interpreter rose from the bed, switched on the transistor radio a little louder, said "I like these things. I must get one," at which the P.M. eyed him coldly and then he began:

"Word was received by Her Majesty's Government in Iota that certain elements in the population were planning treason."

The P.M. waved an impatient hand.

"That is the communiqué for Reuters. Read us the real report."

"Two-for-Three is plannin' to have a bottle-party at the Paradise."

The Minister of Education sat up.

"Bottle party? Bottle party? What is that?"

"A party at which bottles will be thrown," the Interpreter said surprised and cold. The cabinet digested this in silence. The Prime Minister said to the tailor:

"Three buttons in front."

The tailor nodded.

"And put in a slit at the back."

"Slit?"

"Slit."

The cabinet started speaking all at once. The transistor radio played a disco tune about a woman who cried out at night. The Minister of Education tapped out the rhythm. He said to no one in particular, "We must be prepared." The Permanent Secretary for Defence, a hot-headed youth, said, "Call out the army."

They argued over this for some time until the Minister of Defence and if necessary War pointed out that most of the army was on holiday. Then suddenly the P.M. stopped examining the lapel of his jacket and wondering whether he ought to transfer the Saville Row trademark to the new suit he was wearing.

"Gentlemen," he said. He turned off the transistor. "Gentlemen. Has it struck you that this whole business of Independence has come too quickly and too easily? We are the last country in the world to become independent and whether we like it or not we are having it."

The cabinet waited. They were glad that when the Prime Minister spoke to them he avoided his speech-making Latinisms.

"When I remember the old days," the P.M. continued, "soldiers despatched to the Caribbean, bombing in Suez, imprisonments all over the world and so on. It was wonderful! They fought for their freedom. It was a great thing."

The cabinet was beginning to get the drift of the P.M.'s thoughts. "But," the Minister for Public Enlightenment began. "Eh! Ah - you -" He was waved to silence.

"We can't take our seat on the U.N. side by side with countries like Australia . . . " the voice trailed off. "The last colony in the world to become independent!" he ended bitterly.

"What are we to do?" the Permanent Secretary for Defence asked again.

"Don't stop Two-for-Three," the P.M. decided. "Let him come to the Paradise. Let him have his bottle party Blacks to the back. Whites see the light."

This threw the cabinet into uproar. But the P.M. silenced them.

"This is a great day in Iotan history."

He struck a stance as if he were making a speech.

"Its repercussions will echo around the quadruple corners of this terrestrial plane."

He could imagine the cheers of the people. The Minister of Health coughed and spat through the window.

*       *       *

A girl with tight thighs and breasts that moved like bongoes came out of the railway station into the sunshine, the color of powder. Behind her she had left a night during which a wayward train had stopped at the wrong stations at the wrong time and had twice been derailed. A woman had vomited and a man had died. Behind her too were the station policemen waiting to be bribed, railway drivers and guards exchanging endless greetings and passengers who were always sleeping near the rails. She walked up the coal-track that led out to the road. Two idlers watched her go, her suitcase swinging in her left hand, a hand-bag over her right, her bottom moving like maracasses, her small feet in casuals, her face, thin and brown, the color of gravy.

"Hey," she called out to one of the idlers. "Come take my suitcase." The one addressed transferred his chewing-stick to the other side of his mouth. He did not answer. Things were not so bad that one had to work for a woman. She glowered at him and continued. A car slowed down past her stirring up a screen of coal-dust and the driver called out to her. She ignored him, dancing in her passage as if to music.

A small boy rushed against her skirt. His dusty toes pranced agitatedly on the coal-track.

33

"Please Madam make I take yo' load?"

She smiled kindly. She bent down stroking his bald grey head.

"No school?" she asked.

He shrugged his shoulders, placed a dirty band on his head and hoisted up the suitcase. She said, "Straight on to Paradise."

The boy walked on, the suitcase parallel to the road, swinging precariously but never falling. She followed a little quicker now. The kindness had gone out of her eyes; instead a sort of vacancy had replaced it. The afternoon wind crushed her hair.

The Paradise was so called because it approximated very closely to hell on earth. It was early evening and as yet patrons were scarce. However from outside two loudspeakers continued to blare out an infernal noise as record after record discharged itself on to the street.

Inside the Manager sat under an electric fan talking to a fat waitress. All the tables were in the corner, the chairs were still stacked up from the previous night. A solitary tree grew in the center boarded round with barb-wire. Stairs ran up at one end to where on afternoons one could sit under the sky.

"You are late," the Manager was saying to the waitress.

"Yes," she answered weakly as she did every day.

The Manager swore at her. He was a huge man and when he swore the full venom of his words came out like thunder.

"Yes?" he asked, "Yes? Is only yes you know to say? Eh? Answer me."

"No," the waitress said agreeably.

He exploded again.

"No? No? He-e-e-!" He exhaled and turned away in disgust. "Look make you have your sex-life in your leisure period, not in my time."

The waitress agreed again. The Manager said:

"Tomorrow night you know we have a special dance for the Prime Minister? Eh? You no remember?" She did remember.

"Well get this place ready then."

He was going to continue but the waitress was too uncooperative and did not provide a suitable basis for a quarrel, so he turned away again. He sent a table sprawling and walked past a sign stating "No Prostitution" and up to a door marked: "No entrance this way except on business." Behind the door he had heard a noise and hoping for a more agreeable row he bolted through it.

There were about six or seven women behind the door, sitting out in the yard combing one another's hair, washing clothes or eating; they were doing it all very loudly.

34

"By Jesus Christ," he bawled addressing the noise. "Less noise. You no what tomorrow night is? Why you no get ready? Eh?"

They saw he was excited and laughed. He fumed his way to the back and in his anger decided to enter the toilet. He went up a stair where a room with a drain running on one side was parted off into three divisions with wire-mesh. One said "Gents" the other "Ladies" and the third "Manager." He went into the "Ladies."

When he came out he occupied a few minutes in reading a notice that was as bold as it was legendary:

"All bodies caught entering this part of Paradise for unlawful purpose of prostitution will be persecuted."

It was signed by him and underneath he had printed "Manager, Paradise Hotel." He felt proud when he read it. But it still did not bring his good humor. He went past the women again. They had re-started their chatter. Behind them twelve doors stood like sentinels. A woman's voice called out:

"Mister Maninja; make you dey come fo' your rent."

"I no have time now Number Six; tomorrow night na political dance."

"Mister Maninja," Number Six called out, "it no take long with you." She laughed. The Manager appeared indecisive, then he refused to be tempted. He said stolidly, "Tomorrow night na political dance," and went back outside.

In the yard one or two of the tables had been occupied. The loudspeakers continued shouting. The fat waitress had disappeared. In the far corner a girl was sitting. The boy who had walked ahead of her was leaning against the tree with the suitcase on his head. The Manager called to her over his shoulder.

"No more room. No more lodgers."

She got up slowly. Her breasts jerked slightly. Her voice poured out over the tables to where the Manager was.

"What of Number One?"

The Manager spun round.

"Number One?" he began. "God!" he shouted. "It's Dele!" And he started to dance round her, clapping his hands to the music.

She smiled again, a little coldly.

"Tomorrow night na independence dance," he said.

"I know," Dele replied quietly. "That is why I've come. Because of the Prime Minister."

The boy expected a tip but the Manager gave him a cursing and drove him off. He took the suitcase.

"This way," he said leading her up the stairs but looking back all the way at the glimpse of ankle he saw behind him when her legs climbed the steps. He led her into the first room marked Number One. He dumped down the suitcase and started to pull down the mosquito netting.

"No," she said, "Leave it."

Her voice seemed to come from far away. She sat on the bed and her skirt threw itself carelessly over the shape of her thighs. Her ankle bulged slightly where the rim of the bed touched it. He came near her.

"The rent," he whispered huskily, "is payable in advance."

She got up a little haughtily.

"I have no money now. I'm in Number One. Don't forget. Come back tomorrow and you'll get money - nothing else."

She spoke the last words like something disagreeable. He shook his head humbly and got up, moving to the door like a man about to be crucified. She laughed softly, her voice coming from the pillow. "See you later, Mister Manager."

The Manager went out to the loudspeakers and the guests downstairs and the fat waitress and the noise behind the door. He danced round the tree, hawking as he went.

*     *     *

Sunlight fell heavily on dusty toes, cork legs and sweat. Two goats copulated near a Mercedes. The tall heat swam in the sun; shadows of tarmac lay heavy. The policemen exercised their whips and their rights in enforcing Iotan law. The multitude spat and waited respectfully.

Notices hastily written on unpainted brown wood warned the throng: Do not sit there; do not stand here; this is the path of the great man who will soon pass; it is an offense not to watch the procession; do not urinate near the flag post. A wind, ignorant of notices, democratically scattered dust in the faces of the waiting officials. A beggar twitched in the sand and unhopefully coughed. A pickpocket moved about dolefully.

Whenever the Prime Minister travelled he was preceeded by six cars, then he followed in his own car, the latest American model as large as the former three put together. Then he was followed by a few Rolls-Royces, Cadillacs and Mercedes reserved for the younger ministers. The procession usually made its way through the European reservation - no horns please (which nationalism was still to remove) with loud derisive hoots of the horns of cars from various parts of the world. The P.M. himself did not favor the usual

"Popm Popm" on most cars and had mechanics flown out to reverse his own sound to "Pmpo Pmpo." The driver of his own car was oblivious to zebra crossings, halt signs, major road stops or any other obstructions. They were all happy warriors of the road. They knew no speed limit and went along cheerfully at ninety with their occupants behind listening to their radios.

The crowd that usually lined the routes on these occasions was summoned by the police. A few stray prisoners were brought out under guard, a few policemen and soldiers in mufti and anybody who happened to be passing was swiftly roped in and told he could not proceed until the procession had passed. In this way usually a tolerable crowd managed to line the route. Sometimes some section of it might raise an enthusiastic cheer but the Prime Minister usually ignored it, especially as at this particular time the top ten was featuring at the local station.

"What you think the reception will be like?" Sir Ianty asked for about the fifth time.

The driver shifted in the borrowed Mercedes and replied again for the fifth time, "I am sure everyone will be full of jubilation and anticipatory felicitations." He bowed slightly and rubbed his hands. Sir Ianty felt re-assured. He liked hearing the driver talk. As a matter of fact that was why he always had him by his side, since he could get him out of any difficulties with two rubs of his hands and four long words. Sir Ianty never knew how the driver had learnt to speak like that, and often wondered if he invented the words himself. In a way the driver was his speech-writer. And it always worked and so all through they had been together, without anyone suspecting where Sir Ianty obtained his vocabulary.

"I think," Sir Ianty pronounced, as the driver took a bend at sixty, "the first words of my speech today will be what you tell me."

The driver rubbed his hands and said dreamily.

"All men are born equal - that is the inalienable right of homo sapiens." Sir Ianty observed the driver with wonder and committed the words to memory. He would introduce his speech with those words and they would always be sure of a good applause. If only people could remember that Sir Ianty said that all men were equal and therefore it must be so. Then he could be sure of enough money to keep him happy for some time . . .

"But when I use all those big words, you think they understand me?" Sir Ianty asked, abruptly breaking off from his reverie. The driver lovingly caressed his palms and in eloquent reply waved one elegant wrist-watched hand outside the window.

"Of course not," was the reply. "But that is scarcely the salient factor. What is of pre-eminent importance is that, phonologically speaking, it should sound grandiloquent." He brought in his hand from the window and looked at the time.

Sir Ianty of course did not understand, but that did not matter. He nodded his head in agreement. The driver narrowly missed a cow that blocked his path and then he increased his speed. Sir Ianty thought over to himself, "All men are born equal - that is the inalienable right of homo sapiens . . ." over and over again until it started drumming through his head with the sound of the car engine. As he thought to himself the car gathered speed and the needle of the speedometer jerked up higher and higher. The prospect spread itself before them and the sun had colored the grass shiny green; a herdsman drove his cattle across the sunset and below them the town sprawled in an untidy heap. The driver's thoughts were elsewhere, and he could not be expected to realize when he had entered the speed limit area. He moved along at seventy to the tune of the protesting engine and the words that buzzed through his head. Sir Ianty repeated then: "All men are born equal - that is the inalienable right of homo sapiens."

Sir Ianty's thoughts, far from being on the next generation, were actually dwelling on the subject of his safety; he shifted uncomfortably in his seat. He was about to say something when it happened. A goat, which had apparently never heard of "Safety First," decided to cross the road. It was a proud goat, the boldest of the species that Sir Ianty had ever seen, and it crossed the road as no other goat had ever done. It was peacefully browsing in the corner waiting for its next car, since every evening it played a game with other goats called "Make the Car Stop." This game amused it to no end. It would wait until a car was quite near, and would then suddenly dart out as if it were going to cross the road. Then when the car seemed to be slowing down it would pretend to dart back until the car got going again, and then in a slow deliberate way it would start to cross the road. One can easily imagine the confusion that resulted as brakes were hastily applied and passengers were suddenly precipitated forward, and the screech of frightened women as the car stopped. The other goats who always assembled on the other side of the road to watch the antics, were no end pleased with the game and the goat that could stop the greatest number of cars was counted a hero in goat-village. This particular goat which the driver encountered that evening was the present hero (the last one had perished in the speed-limit area under the wheels of a police-van), and that evening he was merely doing routine stuff as the other goats looked on. He could not of course have been expected to know that his present opponent in his little game was Sir Ianty's driver and that his thoughts were far away. So what happened was that the goat went through its little maneuver, which the driver did not observe, and when it was doing its slow walk across, both occupants were abruptly jolted into the present tense when the car collided with it. The goat moaned softly, threw up its forelegs and fell. The championship title once more fell vacant. The driver twiddled his fingers as the car came to a halt, and rubbed his hands expressively.

"I am inclined to infer," he pronounced, "that as a result of our profound cogitations, we have collided with a quadruped ruminant."

Sir Ianty, as usual, did not understand, but he guessed rightly that this meant they had hit a goat. He got out of the car.

By then the deserted road had become full of at least a dozen people who began to shout and argue loudly. Sir Ianty began to curse himself that this should have happened.

"Na who goat be this?" Sir Ianty shouted above the uproar. No one answered. He tried two African languages, English and some bad Italian, but the uproar only seemed to grow in volume. Then a tall man with well developed muscles and a rather large head, came up and said:

"I be headman. What was your speed?" Sir Ianty almost exploded. He remembered that in a peculiar way, at counting time, these people mattered. Instead he said to the man, continuing in the dialect, "Make I see owner for goat, give him money."

The headman looked at him, then he said slowly scratching his large head, "I be headman, Make you give me."

Sir Ianty refused and that was his mistake. The headman said something to the crowd and they started shouting again. After a few seconds they seemed to be getting worked up and Sir Ianty retreated back into his car. The hostile mob stood round the car, blocking his path. Desperately he wondered what he ought to do. An irrelevant refrain kept going through his head: "All men are born equal. All men are born equal. All men are born equal." Then luckily a local authority policeman arrived.

He listened to all the headman said and shook his head, then he listened to the crowd and shook his head, and then to Sir Ianty, but he did not shake his head:

"You go catch plenty trouble fo' this. Let me see your driving license." Sir Ianty groaned inwardly. This was the end. If the policeman knew who he was he would be so afraid he would let him go. But that would solve nothing. He said goodbye to his beautiful speech on equal rights and closed his eyes. But he had forgotten the driver. The latter was saying to the police-officer:

"My dear Sir, this gentleman has recently arrived from England, and is wending his way to independence celebrations."

"No hear the thing you say," the policeman said stolidly.

The driver climbed down. It was the first and last time that Sir Ianty heard him use the dialect.

"This," he pronounced disdainfully, tossing his hands in anguish, "na England man and he is a committee of one."

The policeman bowed and stepped back two paces. He said something to the crowd, and when the head-man argued he took out his notebook threateningly. As if by magic the crowd dispersed. The policeman said to Sir Ianty:

"I too sorry to interrupt your travelling."

The driver nodded distantly and murmured, "It is regrettable."

The driver started the car and drove off slowly. After he got a little way Sir Ianty thanked the driver. Then he said to him:

"You know I will change that speech. I will tell them that only sometimes some men are equal." Sir Ianty said nothing. He kept a strict eye on the speedometer.

When they arrived at a railway crossing the driver stopped. Sir Ianty took time off from listening to the "Topmost Top Ten" to ask, "Eh? What did you stop for?"

"A train desires to pass," the driver replied.

"Don't you think we had enough trouble for one day?"

He sat in annoyed silence for some seconds.

"That man said, Sir, it is a molasses train and that it waits for nobody."

"What man? Open the gates," the Prime Minister bawled a little louder.

The Interpreter got out of the Prime Minister's car and gave the gateman five cents. This immediately activated him and he rushed down the line, red lamp swinging, almost throwing himself in front of the engine. He had now recognized the power of the Prime Minister; five cents is not a small sum. The train braked, the rum waited, the gates were thrown open again and Sir Ianty Pakeman proceeded with party.

When they arrived at the Paradise Sir Ianty was not in a very good mood and he ignored the twin strip of linoleum provided for him to walk on and made his silent way upstairs to the special table. His entourage followed. The loudspeaker increased its volume. In front of them the barman, in between serving drinks and increasing the loudspeaker volume, was staring at the newcomers. They ordered their drinks. "Bitter lemon for me," the Prime Minister said sourly.

The Minister of Education, who always felt that these occasions called for some display of intelligence, started a discussion:

"What we need is a University."

"Who will attend it with half the population illiterate?" asked one of the two Permanent Secretaries. No one answered his question as it was considered foolish.

"What is a University?" the Minister for Public Enlightenment asked sleepily. The Prime Minister felt better now. As a man who had travelled, he was in a position to explain.

"Ivy League, Big Ten and small ones - three different types."

The waitresses started serving drinks and for a few seconds nobody said anything as sucking noises began emptying the glasses.

"A toast," the Prime Minister said rising. He was feeling better.

"But what will we teach there?" the Permanent Secretary asked again.

There was some consternation. The Prime Minister again came to the rescue.

"A University," he said sitting down, "is like a primary school except they have bigger buildings and more holidays. In a country like Iota we need to teach the main subjects to a higher level. We will naturally devote some time to languages like English, and Science like Arithmetic, and Poetry which is the singing and understanding of party propaganda will also be studied."

The loudspeaker again rose in volume and drowned all conversation - the opposition started arriving. When the Rev. Two-for-Three was told that the Prime Minister was above, he asked the Manager.

"By what right does that man sit above me?"

"You sit there too, Sah," the Manager compromised.

"We are not on the same level," Two-for-Three replied bitterly.

His party sat downstairs around the tree. The legendary notices were all around and the door through which entrance was forbidden was wide open.

"The plan," Two-for-Three said to his shadow Minister of War, "is for you to start an argument."

The Minister of War understood. "And there the bottle party starts. Hold one of his Ministers for hostage."

Beer was served. His thoughts became intoxicated. He saw himself as the future leader of a great Iotan people. After half a bottle, Two-for-Three said,

"It is only fair we Blacks should govern."

The Shadow Interpreter agreed and wrote it down in a white notebook he always carried around for the occasion, entitled "Thoughts of the Leader of a Developing Nation."

"We must wait," he whispered to no one. "Until they are drunk. Then we strike."

Music raged round the tables, under the chairs and people's feet started twitching. Other people came in and sat round. A man started dancing up the stairs. The Manager left.

"The Whites are from Europe," Two-for-Three, the Prime Minister in Opposition pronounced, "and that is a country which Euraf thus named because he had to call several million Whites by some name."

The Shadow Interpreter took out his notebook, changed his mind and drained his glass instead. "Whisky," he called out.

The Manager danced his way up the stairs; his heavy body rolled to the rhythm that the loudspeakers noised out. The melody brought him to the door of Number One. It was half open and he knocked softly.

"Are you ready?"

"Yes. Tell Sir Ianty I'm here in Number One waiting."

The Manager laughed. "Ha! You t'ink the Prime Minister go come look fo' you."

She slammed the door. He stood there for a moment, walked soberly up a few more steps. What should he do? When he came to the top he saw the sky and the stars like yo-yos hanging down. When in doubt he always went to the lavatory. He did, but this time he knew what to do midway in his reflections on the ladies. He would tell the Prime Minister. It would be a good joke. Make the great Dele know herself for the common whore she was.

He went up to the tables slowly. A record noisily itched its way to silence on the loudspeakers. For ten seconds there was silence in the Iotan night. The Governor and his party started arriving be-jacketed for the occasion. The Manager hastily went to the top of the stairs bowed and said,

"This way, Sah." The Governor followed military style, flanked on one side by his wife, on the other by his aide-de-camp.

"Good evening," the Governor said amiably as he passed Sir Ianty Pakeman's table.

This was ignored for some seconds and then the Interpreter whispered something into the less drunk ear. Sir Ianty Pakeman glanced up, remembered not to get up in time and said: "Nocturnal felicitations."

42

The Governor passed his way.

"What shall we do about the glasses?" the Governor's wife whispered.

"What glasses?"

"You know they'll serve us something - oral V.D., T.B., herpes, you can get the lot here."

"O God!" the Governor groaned. He straightened himself: "Never mind! Colonial office orders! Whatever the cost."

They sat down and a waitress brought drinks. A fly obligingly fell into His Excellency's glass. He was about to toast the health of Iota, fly and all, when the waitress hastily switched glasses.

The Manager felt more confident now the music was surging round his soles.

"Sah!" he said.

Sir Ianty's eyelids flickered. The Manager addressed the Interpreter. The Interpreter addressed the Prime Minister. Sir Ianty staggered to his feet.

"Who?"

"Dele, Sah, in Number One. Say she want see you," the Manager stuttered.

This was certainly not the reception he expected. The Prime Minister looked sharply at him and started hastily walking away.

# CHAPTER 4

Pietro was more than a little nervous when he got into the dark hotel room. It was one thing getting past the eyes of the desk clerk and trying to look as if he had booked in earlier, another problem going up the elevator with an elderly couple who kept giggling, and quite another as he got out on the seventh floor. He started to make his way down the corridor, trying to look in as unobtrusive a manner as possible for the right door. God only knows what the hell he could have been letting himself in for. He was game for almost anything, but at times there were conservative shutters which were like obstacles to him.

Three knocks and he was quietly let in. His eyes were blinded by the darkness and he could make out very little. Pietro's heart kept pounding. There was something about this that was right and crazy and ridiculous and all wrong at the same time. But he had come hadn't he? And he was going to go through with it. Try anything once, he used to say. He began undressing.

Through the crack near the ledge where the blinds did not fit too well, he could make out the lights in the streets below. Not too late, Pietro boy, he thought to himself. Haul your ass out of here. This is some crazy mixed-up thing.

"Coming in?" It was a woman's voice, sounding from what must have been the foot of the bed. He didn't reply. Instead he tugged off his shorts, got in and hauled the blanket over him.

She was under there, just near his feet, and now that his eyes were getting accustomed to the dark, he could make out the faint outline of a man's head on the pillow on the other side of her. As he pushed his feet farther down, he felt the transfer of a body from one side to the other. The man's head was still the same place, motionless, like something that had been forgotten and left hanging. He felt her wet lips on his toes and he jerked with a sensation that was

45

both pleasurable and painful. The feet that were near him, which he could not see, rolled from side to side and he too began to kiss them; warm, firm heels that were smooth and an instep around which he curved his tongue. The feet stopped turning now and were very still and the toes had the tangy taste of salt. As he went deeper in, he felt a stab at his navel and he gave a long involuntary sigh, as if he were tasting some fresh fruit that no one else in the world knew. The head on the other side of the feet was still motionless, and as he went round the ankle-bone and touched the very edge of her leg, he thought he heard the sound of cable cars and bells in the distance.

She moved again and soon he was in complete darkness; even the window had disappeared; instead there was the clean smell of bedclothes and the taste of tiny drops of perspiration between the thighs. Her head was still now. He only felt the soft caress of his toe and the occasional jab of his toenail against her gum. There, he thought, he could be forever and never come, with his neck muscles strained and his nose taking in the fragrance of an odor that he seemed to eat with his nostrils, and which slowly worked its way into his guts. He reached out with his left hand and felt the hairy thighs of the quiet man on her side. At first some of his doubts came back and for a split second he almost jerked his hand back; but he let it stay there and the man slid himself easily and softly into the arch of Pietro's damp palm.

They never spoke about it. But everytime he drove past Nob Hill, everytime he heard the cable cars crunch their way and grind to a halt or come with a clamour of bells, Pietro remembered. Like now. He was leaving the lights of the bay behind him and moving slowly past the hill and he remembered. He slowed down near a mail-box and tried to wedge some books in for Stephan, muttered under his breath and came out of his car. You always had to do something surgical with a mail box to get a decent sized package in. He put his right hand in and held it open, and slowly, with a kind of grace, he slid the books in with his left hand. He could feel the books, standing almost upright before he let them go and they fell softly, with the ease of flesh into place.

"I sent him the books," he told Dele after he had mixed himself a drink at her place.

"What?" she was showering and he had to yell back.

He heard the water that was bursting out and raining down on the tiles and in his head those bells, the grate of the street-car and then silence. "I got a letter from him today," she said as she came and sat opposite him round the small table in the kitchenette. She lit a cigarette, changed her mind, put it out, got up in her green bath towel, rummaged round inside and came back, cupping her hands around what she was rolling. As she sat down she crossed her legs and licked the paper smoothly, with a final upward stroke that left it tight and erect. He shoved her an ash tray and lit one of the two candles she had on the table.

"Talked about the life there. Sounds pretty dull the way he tells it." She put her fingers round the plug of her hairdryer and, bending over her chair, she pushed in the plug easily.

"You want to?"

Yes. He liked to blow dry her hair. He used to tease her about it. They make funny niggers where you come from. She used to laugh. "All sizes. If I lived there still with my parents I would be the *mulata,*" she replied once. "You know sensuous and seductive and live a happy life with a tragic end." The strands of her hair would come up, one at a time it seemed to him, and perch as erect as an aroused penis and then fall down. He would smooth it down with his hand. When he blew her hair from the back of her neck all of part of it would seem to be in turmoil, to stand up or to want to stand up all at once and, if for a moment, he turned the dryer away, they all fell down as suddenly. She was young then, he knew. Maybe when you get older, it's not as straight, as erect. Maybe old people are weak, too weak for the head-job he was now giving her. Perhaps their scalps were soft and the hair, no longer fluffy, was thin and sparse. Perhaps you blew and nothing happened. There were no arches which rose up to defend themselves against you, no pillars you could erect and then clutch them to prevent them from falling down. All the life had been eaten out of an old woman's head, leaving her with crazy memories of things that she wished had happened.

"Do you feel he's coming back?" he asked her softly, stooping and peering over the corner of those rising hairs to the flickering light of the candle. She massaged the stem of the candle with thoughtful, clean strokes. She didn't reply. He continued. "Maybe that's silly. He said it was for nine months."

And Pietro had remembered when they went out to the airport to see Stephan off. To the end Stephan had repeated to Pietro, "Nine months - that's not long, is it?"

"You can have - "

"Ha! Ha! Such an entertaining child. A real treasure to his momma," Stephan had laughed at him. "Yes I know you can have a child in nine months."

47

And then he was still and said nothing more until they got to the airport and Dele was helping him find his coat and he had grumbled, "I've got all the wrong clothing," or something like that and Dele had replied, "Keep the wrong clothing on," and he had smiled, quietly, as he always did.

"Look," Stephan remarked suddenly. "Don't come in. It's not a funeral. Go off and do something I would like. Go to the wharf, you know. Think about me when you crack the first crab, before you gobble up the sour bread - " And he had kissed them both right there outside. That was Stephan. Kissed them both as lovingly on their lips and embraced them for a long time. Then he had walked in and turned away from them as if they had never existed and they were left there on the dismal sidewalk with the porters and the cabdrivers and people hurrying past. Dele had shrugged her shoulders and got back in the car and Pietro had driven them both back. And they did exactly what Stephan had wanted them to do. They went to Allioto's and took a table near the ocean and looked over the bay and ate bread and drank wine and said nothing. And he remembered thinking how wrong Stephan had been; it was a damn funeral!

Dele shook her hair and got up: "Talks about a boy-priest." Half of what she had been smoking was in the ash-tray. She stopped near the bedroom door. "What's it tonight? Allioto's?" She usually had a way of answering her own questions. Perhaps this was why it was so difficult to have that easy relationship he had with most people, where you talk backwards and forth until you tire each other out and expose every bit of you. She never did. She always had something on, those beads round her neck, or something. "I'm not naked," she would say after. "Not really naked with these beads on."

And she had never been. Even on that first night when Stephan's call had brought Pietro down to the hotel and into bed, Pietro had felt those damn beads round her neck. They had only brushed against part of his thigh then, but later on that was how he knew it was her. They were red and white beads which she wore at all times. She never even took them off, not even to have a bath.

"Shango beads," she had told him one night when he dared question her.

He dug in a little deeper, "What are Shango beads?"

"Oh you Americans - sorry Italians - you know so little about anything. Don't you know - the god of lightning and thunder? When Blacks came to the New World they changed his name to Santa Barbara - "

"A woman? - "

"So?" her eyes were searching. "What does it matter? Did it matter?" That was all. He remembered when it did not, when his left hand had reached out and felt Stephan lying next to her, Stephan's manhood as tall as a pole.

48

Dele came out wearing trousers and a blouse with a handknitted design. Her chain hung down over her. "He made me remember my own boy-priest. I'm going to have to visit him soon." Outside he started the car and pulled it smoothly out of the driveway. She rolled up her side of the window and the prickly points of hair became soft and lay down.

"My santéro priest - it's my birthday."

"Wasn't your birthday about six months ago?"

"Not that one. My real birthday. When I was initiated into santería. I missed going last year because of Stephan . . . " She let it trail off. Pietro did not understand. Why did she have to see this priest, this santéro, on her birthday that wasn't her birthday? What did they do? Peculiar niggers, he thought, from where she comes from. He was feeling a little bold that night, so he said, "Oh some wild African magic," and regretted it because she was only silent for a moment and continued with her own trend of thinking. "It's really strange. I bet Stephan doesn't understand what the hell is happening. I mean about the boy-priest. He probably thinks it's all very funny. It's funny peculiar all right. He walks into a strange country by mistake and out of the blue he meets a priest - "

"Dele dear you're not making much sense."

"I know. I know. Do I ever to you?"

When they got to the restaurant, he looked round, found somewhere to park and they trudged upstairs. The bay, the goddamn bay. It was even pointing the wrong way. But something about this town will always be a part of Stephan. They had been there too long together and this strange girl from another country was what Stephan had left behind for him. Stephan never wrote Pietro. He wrote Dele for both of them. She told him what he was to do. Buy books and send them. He went out and did that. Bought books and sent them. "Are you religious, Dele?" he asked when they were seated at the same table they had taken that night when Stephan went away. The waiter hovered over them with the menu.

"What the hell you think I've been talking about? she asked impatiently. The wine had come and he poured it reverently into her glass and he filled his own.

"No. The name," he murmured. "Do you think he's a martyr?"

She sipped softly, her tongue lingering on the rim of glass for a second too long, "He's not selfish enough to be a martyr. Martyrs are basically very selfish people, concerned with history and what some fool a hundred years later will think. Stephan does not understand a hundred years later. He's a today boy."

49

Pietro thought that this was true. Stephan had always existed for the moment and projected himself in a single moment of time. When you were with Stephan that was all you wanted. When you weren't you missed his accumulations of single moments. It was as if he had the capacity to stretch life out and slice it into segments like the sour dough they were now eating. But *he* had done the slicing. *You* ate. The taste lingered in *your* mouth. For a moment or two as they chewed in silence he wanted to ask her about the meaning of their first night together in a dark hotel room. Was it part of how she saw the world? Shango or Santa Barbara - man and woman at one and the same time - what did it matter? Or was it Stephan's wish for the impulsive moment of ecstasy?

"Me," Dele said when the food came. "I've got a definite feeling for history. Now could not be without then. I am what I am because of all they were."

He was about to say, "They who?" when the waiter came back saying was everything all right? Did they like the bread and wine? Would they like some more? Dele said no and the waiter drifted off to worry someone else.

"In this crazy place I couldn't live without that." She brought up a forkful of food, like an offering, to her mouth, and her mouth opened and she took it in and slowly she began to seemingly roll it from side to side. He watched her as he ate his own crab, and the little clutch of her throat had told him when she had swallowed.

"And it is the priests who keep this alive, who tell us who we are and what we are. Without that boy-priest, griot, santéro, call him what you will, this would be one poor lost girl, not knowing who the hell she is."

Pietro felt he ought to speak. "Hell I *know* who I am. I'm Italian, twenty eight, I live in San Francisco, I hope to finish medical school, I've got a job and I'm in love with you."

Dele laughed softly. "Oh? I thought we were making pillow talk. So we've been at it like it's going out of fashion for the past two months - so what?"

"Well Dele," Pietro was a little angry now, "at least I think that you belong to me and - "

"Nobody belongs to anybody. That much my religion tells me. Martyrs do not belong to their causes, people do not belong to their bodies and it takes a hell of a lot of stupidity to think that you belong to a place, a color, a name, just because it looks like that to you." She had finished eating and now folded her napkin crosswise on the table. "Only the priests can *know*, because they are the only ones who kept the head count."

The waiter fluttered over them again and Pietro said, "Yes bring the check," as his eyes wandered round the lights of the bay. He thought when he looked at the heave of Dele's breasts and the curve of her chin which seemed to peek over her blouse, that he heard the sound of the cable cars and their steady headlong plunge from hilltop to green oceanside. Outside he asked, "You're not cross with me, are you?" and she shook her head, and for one moment he wanted to kiss her, but he knew she would have pushed him off. For a second or two he looked directly at her when he got inside the car. "You're one complicated lady aren't you?" No reply as he turned on the ignition. He was even afraid to ask her if they should go directly back to her apartment. After all she always told him if he should or should not. That was the territory of their relationship from jump street. From the first night, after Stephan had gone, and after the bread and wine she had said, "Now my body" as if she had been carrying out orders - holy orders. And she had bathed him with the love of a mother and the sweet hands of a lover and rinsed his face with warm water and massaged his back with soap. Then he had washed her feet, rubbing the ankles delicately and letting the towel soak up the water from her dripping toes. She had left his hair wet and sat on the edge of the tub and said something about vine leaves. His hair smelt of vine leaves, not bay like Stephan's temples. But later, as he lay under her on the living room floor, his head jammed next to the television, she had called on Stephan and collapsed sobbing over him. He heard the bells, the scrape of the streetcars and, in the distance, perhaps the fading sound of an airplane.

Now when he was back on the road he noticed that she too had lowered her window and the wind ransacked her hair and kept it almost vertical. This was their second month together and every time they had lain down, Stephan was with them. She called on Stephan, cursed him, was sweet to him, made him promises. Pietro's body was a thing she used, a medium he once thought, for her to have Stephan enter her. He had wondered if she even needed him, because one night after she had given him a key he had gone upstairs and found her in bed, her eyes bright in the darkness, her hands under the blanket and he heard his own voice and Stephan's and her actual groans from the bed. Half afraid, he had turned the light on and said, "What the fuck?" And she had gotten up quickly, like a child caught doing something naughty, and taken the cartridge out of the taperecorder and disappeared into the bathroom. Only then did he know that their first meeting with Stephan in the hotel room had been taped from start to finish like a cheap porno movie. She refused to talk about it, hid the tape and adamantly objected to his questions. So he had come to accept the relationship, such as it was. He was her plaything to conjure back the

51

memory of Stephan, and neither his body nor, in the final analysis, the tape mattered. With her acute sense of history she had placed one joyous moment forever in a capsule and she used it when and how often she liked.

At the second stoplight, Dele said, "I've been pregnant since last month." He almost clutched his throat. Stephan had been gone for over two months. "For Ianty, Stephan or Pietro..." she concluded irreverently he thought, and when he got to her apartment she got out, closed the car door softly with her back to him and went slowly in, as if dragging an enormous burden.

*       *       *

To get to the Post Office, Stephan had to leave the area where they were housed, drive on a sandy road for about a mile and turn right. After the few shops in the town and the houses behind the railway line, he drove past the Emir's palace and swung left into the Post Office. When he got out, he realized just how hot it was. He and his shadow sweated their way across the street to the other side. The Post Office was a one story building that seemed to have just sprung up, out of nowhere. Outside a letter-writer was plying a busy trade, seated on a stool, in a bamboo enclosure with an open door, engaged in the process of translating and writing at the same time. For a small fee those of his clients who were unable to read could have their letters written in English, and then they would go up to the window at the Post Office and dispatch them.

"To oversea," the man ahead of him was repeating loudly. "Think say you never hear 'bout oversea?"

"Which part oversea," the Post Office clerk behind the screen was yelling. "Them get all kind oversea. England oversea, America oversea, France oversea..."

The man ahead of Stephan looked bewildered. Stephan peeked over and read out what the letter-writer had just inscribed.

"America," he said to the Post Office clerk.

The clerk looked at him for sometime. "Na you who dey send dis letter? I no ask you which side letter dey go. Na dis man I ask. Mek he tell me and I go give am the stamp."

The man said, "'Merica," in a bold voice and the clerk yelled, "Bring money," grabbed it, then tossed him the stamps and some change.

"I've come for some books," Stephan said. He retrieved a crumpled notice from his pocket and passed it under the grille. The clerk said, "Oh, you're from America - Yankee?" Suddenly polite, his manner had abruptly changed. Gone was the bullying and the one-upmanship. "Thank you," from him as Stephan passed the notice and there was a "Here you are Sir," as he handed Stephan the parcel of books which Pietro had sent.

Stephan walked back into the sunshine, pulling his shadow with him, past the letter-writer's makeshift office, past a woman padding round on her knees capped with car-tire rubber soles. He got back into his car, tossed the books behind him and started moving. Two schoolboys crossed the street, white shirts and khaki uniforms, books under their arms. He drove past the palace again, but this time he had to do it very slowly for he observed that a crowd of people had formed outside the gates. There was traffic in front and behind him and he slowed down in the sticky heat. The schoolboys passed him again and he heard one say to the other, "Emir Ahmed is dead." The other did not seem to be too upset. He laughed, but they had walked on before Stephan had heard what his reply was.

Finally the traffic cleared and he was able to move on again slowly until he came to the turning that led him to the direction in which he was living. It was almost like a different world. He had heard that before the country was independent, this part had been termed the European Reservation. The houses were high on a hill and caught the sea-breeze. At nights he could see the harbor and the lights of the dock. If he stretched his imagination a little it reminded him of San Francisco, except it was all pointing in the wrong direction.

Later at home Stephan told James that he was eating out that night. He was going to Frost's house. Some Americans were in town and they were all getting together. Life is a bitch, he thought. Here I'm an American, to Frost, to the guy in the post office. It was just like we didn't have that little difference of opinion back home. You know, when some of us were niggers? Damn strange! And sitting here on this terrace looking out again at sundown and waiting for the schoolchildren to come past, he was thinking, yes and why the hell not? We've lived in the damn country just about as long as anybody else except the Indians, so why not?

"Tea Sah?" James again. Stephan put down one of the books he was attempting to look at which Pietro had sent him. Instead of replying, he asked, "Say James where's that crazy guy you brought over here the other day?"

"The priest, sah?"

"Priest? Yeah, the boy-priest." Stephan laughed. Priest?

James pointed and Stephan noticed that once more he had almost missed the procession of children who went past his house every evening. The sun was already behind Frost's house but he could still make them out. At the head was Sarki, clad in white, his head high, looking only forward. The children followed as they usually did, chanting.

"What the hell's the matter with him?" he asked James but there was no reply. James had vanished with the sun.

The talk at Frost's house was about Emir Ahmed's death. There was some guy from the local university, an Englishman, who seemed to be an authority on the subject. Before dinner, he held forth.

"There'll be trouble now," he said. "You see Ahmed was a pretender to the emirate and he died childless. The real successor is a man from the south. They're looking for him."

"What does he rule?" Frost asked in his whimsical way.

The Englishman's eyes opened wide. "Dear boy, you Americans! The entire state - "

. "I thought you people ruled 'em," Frost cut in dryly.

"Up to a point. Do you think the English could get anything done here without the help of the locals? Look," he seemed to be getting excited, "take the work of governing, the civil service, the courts, the local councils - who do you think does that?"

"So all *you* folks do is take care of the diamonds and sugar and make sure they keep each other in place." Frost was acid. "*We* build the roads."

"Yes," was the snappy rejoinder. "A bit like Puerto Rico, old man."

"Boys, boys," Mrs. Frost came in. "Don't let's get on to politics now." She had a double chin, was a plump matronly woman and seemed to grow paler the longer she remained in Africa. Frost had managed to retain his figure, but then he didn't have the problem of rearing those terrible children.

They sat down to dinner and servants appeared and disappeared with different courses. For some reason one of the Frost Brats had been put near him and she struck up a conversation.

"You work for my father?"

"We work for the same company," Stephan replied.

She giggled. Couldn't have been more than fourteen, he thought. Must have taken her some getting used to this. This thing about us all being Americans. The guests were two Peace Corps women who had been living up country and whom Frost had discovered one day in town. Members of what Stephan called the Death Corpse - one Black, one White. Stephan supposed their hearts were in the right places. After all no need to leave Mummy and Momma, Daddy and Poppa and come out here for that kind of bread if they

54

didn't believe in something. They seemed to be quite good friends too; they lived together on a school compound and the White one taught Biology, the Black one History.

"My students are real darlings," the Black one was saying. A chorus replied. "What way out shit is this? Like an effing circus. Why is she pulling that act? Momma know she talk so?"

"Oh yes," from the White one. "Much better motivated than our home kids. They want to learn."

"Are you off on vacation?" piped the other one of the terrible Frost bites.

"No," the Black history teacher answered. "As you know the Emir is dead, so we came with them all for the funeral rites."

Sounded so earnest too, he thought. It was bad enough for the other one but the Black one behaved as though she had lost a blood relative. The Englishman began his rundown again about who begat whom and where and why. Seemed like old Ahmed was a clever schemer and had managed with the help of the British to seize power from some guy near Mohammed. Mohammed died mysteriously, but his wife Shade had escaped. This was what the fracas was about. Crazy stuff!

"I've got my class working on the whole background as a project," the Black history teacher told him over liqueurs. He had got himself near her. Not bad looking. A little on the skinny side but fine lips. She wore an Afro and said no thanks she didn't smoke and she was Cecily Dawn, what's your name?

There's one thing for sure that colored folk do anywhere, even stateside. When we meet we wanna know you, who's your momma, where you from, which school you been to, and who's your main man. But this crazy chick wasn't getting into any of this jazz. It was like she was saying to him: Nigger I know what you doing. You trying to label me. But the White man come and do that a long time ago and that's as far as you getting. You got my name. Work from there. Right now I'm a teacher, with little African charges, in a little African village and that once upon a time jive is bull. She would probably have said it more elegantly. But this very same child was still raving and ranting about *her* school, *her* children, *her* project. It was as if she were saying that the good Lord had done nothing but good for her in striking poor Emir What's-his-name dead, so that *her* students at *her* school would have *her* project to carry out.

He thought of Pietro. Pietro had this theory about having a hundred shots and maybe you'll hit a bull's eye. Pietro, quiet as a mouse, pursued this neat little game and went all over Frisco spreading crabs when he wasn't eating

55

them. Would Pietro have gone the whole way with this one? Asked her, you know, bold as can be, asked her, could he have some pussy please? And sometimes when the percentage was right Pietro got it; sometimes not. But what do you do with a pretentious m.f. in a foreign country acting like (a) she didn't have no tail, (b) wasn't giving no tail nohow, and (c) wanted to be admired for her fine mind.

"I'm really interested in what happened to Emir Mohammed's wife, Queen Shade. I would love, just love, to work on her."

"Oh?" What the fuck are you supposed to say? There you are being your sweet, Black self and this bitch is standing there shooting garbage. Carry on!

"You see," she had the attention of the whole room now; even the English authority was silent. "Queen Shade escaped from the palace with their son, the grandson of Sarif Badian and Queen Abu. The descendants of Queen Shade and her child, whatever his name, would have been the rightful rulers of the emirate."

The ghastly Frost children, after harassing the servants, quarrelled their way to their rooms. Mrs. Frost smiled a "Goodnight dears" and received no reply. Cecily Dawn droned on, "The Emir who died today is the third generation of the Ahmed dynasty, Emir Ahmed the third. It's like seeing my own father die."

Perhaps he was not to blame her unduly. This was after all her moment of glory. She was with something that she felt part of, however hazy. What wasn't clear she could invent. Coming from her it sounded real and pressing. Screwed up child, what would your momma say now? You go and adopt yourself a genuine dead African daddy. And the White chick was trying to get in on the act too, not by saying anything but by basking in the glow of what her traveling companion said. Just as if when the Black history teacher, Cecily Dawn spoke, Prince Ahmed the third was waiting outside for her White friend on a dark charger, ready to take her into his castle to perform unspeakable black deeds. What would your White Mummy say to that, you rash little darling? She would place Emir Ahmed the third's butt securely on his black charger, reverse his gears, call the cops and send him back to the ghetto where all good Black folks live. And she would close the blinds, lock up her lily-white daughter and they would all live happily ever after.

# PART II

*The earth never grows fat*

**from an Ngoni Burial song.**

*Say in few words, not lengthening out thy speech,*
*knew'st thou the edicts which forbade these things?*

**Sophocles: Antigone.**

*Speak and tell us, tell us quickly;*
*how we may escape the ghastly?*

**Goethe: Faust.**

# CHAPTER 5

This is the song that the griots sang. Near an old wall of the Emir's palace, sang to the sound of the funeral drum, the whistle of the harp, the rattle of gourd and the tintinnabulation of *kora* and *belafong*. This is the song that the griots sang, to the crowds of mourners outside the palace, to the children who looked on wistfully, understanding some or none at all, to the beggars, parasites, the lame and the deformed in the dust. This is the song that the griots sang.

*"Every neighbor is my brother is my sister, hear oh hear! Every brother, every sister is my neighbor, hear oh hear! And it came to pass that in the kingdom of Sarif Badian there came bitter times, when the vultures wheeled round the palace smelling death and the destruction in his house. Because he had fallen, fallen beneath the hoofmarks of a mere princeling, thus his offspring must suffer for the deep wound of shame that had been inflicted on them.*

*Mohammed, his son, was a man bold in his stride and with fiery eyes. Praises be to Allah for Mohammed his son was a man of valor, of great courage! And it came to pass that when Prince Ahmed the first came to see him seeking his sister's hand in marriage, Emir Mohammed set him a task to see how worthy he was of the hand of Princess Farina. And the task was this: Emir Mohammed saith unto him, 'Behold I will ascend to the roof top of my castle, aye to the very heights. And for three nights shall I slumber there. No woman shall comfort me, neither shall I have the blessing of those who seek counsel of me.*

*'And it shall be your lot to seek me out, thrice, Aye thou too must climb to the very top of this castle and find me. Three nights shall I hide from thee and thou must find me, for is it not said that the true seeker shall find that which is sought? Then shalt thou come down after each seeking to my ministers, the*

*attendants, and report what thou hast seen. Be it bird, beast or man, phantom or fig-leaf, thou shouldst truly answer and say what thou hast seen. And if, at the end of the third night on the rising up of sun, my attendants still do not hear from thee what it is thou seekest, if thou cannot still say indeed what is the truth thou seekest, then shall I know that this is a sign from Allah that thou art no more deserving of my sister than the horses that graze in the shadows of my field.'*

*And Prince Ahmed the Proud One, agreed, saying, 'Verily for three nights shall I seek thee on the rooftop of thy palace. On each night shall I tell thy ministers by a sign what I have seen and Allah in his goodness will reveal to all what I have done.'*

*After they had spoken thus, Prince Ahmed, the Proud One, and Sarif Mohammed, the Wayward, broke kola-nut and agreed that should Prince Ahmed be found knowing in the sign of Allah, thus would all be revealed and he would marry Farina, the sister of Emir Mohamed. Otherwise he would leave and never return.*

*On the first night, Emir Mohammed arose and forbade anyone to accompany him, not even his Clown nor his Interpreter, and climbed by the back of the palace wall and rolled out his mat and prayed and then lay down to slumber. Nor did he know that Prince Ahmed had plotted in his heart to kill him and take away his emirate and marry his sister and thus call himself the rightful inheritor of the sandals of Sarif Badian.*

*So it was with a dagger that Prince Ahmed sought him that first night, such a dagger as men slay sheep for sacrifice at the time of the holy feasts. Prince Ahmed sought him alone, for he feared to tell another of his evil intent. And behold, as Prince Ahmed ascended the wall of the castle, suddenly the roof was plunged into darkness and the moon did not show itself. All night Prince Ahmed sought Emir Mohammed's body in the darkness, but he found it not, and in the morning, when he heard his own companions harkening unto him, he answered back. And when he came down he gave to the attendants of Emir Mohammed a piece of bread which a wayward crow had let fall. And they looked at him but said nought.*

*The next night, fearing for his own life and knowing the evil which lay in his own heart, Prince Ahmed went up with one of his own trusted companions. And their mission was the same; to kill the good and holy man, Emir Mohammed, who daily said his prayers to Allah and who kept the month of Ramadan, fasted and gave alms to the poor. And again as these two men sought him by night, they could not find his body. A swift wind rose up, verily*

*like the Harmattan, which blows in the cool months, and burned their lips
and their fingers with grains of desert sand. And they were sore distraught
and sat near a corner till morning. There they found a flask of palm oil with
which they rubbed their feet for they were in pain. In the morning they came
down and Prince Ahmed, not knowing what it meant, gave the palm oil which
remained to the attendants.*

*With one voice the attendants rose up and said: This can have but one
meaning. For Ahmed hath first taken the very bread of which we eat, and now
the palm oil with which our words are seasoned. He is a man, they cried out in
one voice, who would seek to destroy both our prince, Emir Mohammed, and
then take away our words from us, binding up this land in a most terrible
silence, imposing himself on us, forbidding us freedom. And they were sore
afraid. One rose from amongst them and said: 'Harken ye to me. The will of
Allah hath not yet been fulfilled. Three nights must we tarry till the rising up
of sun on the fourth day, and each man will know in his heart what it is he
must do.'*

*Then, behold, on the third night rain fell in great abundance. And the
courtyard of the emirate was flooded and cattle and horses stood deep in the
flood. Prince Ahmed with two companions sought again all night for Emir
Mohammed. He was still seeking to do his evil deed and destroy the Emir and
thus bring down the house of Sarif Badian. But they found him not, and in the
morning when they returned, Prince Ahmed could only give to the attendants
a cupfull of water and now they were sure and saw in this man the very means
of their destruction.*

*May all praises be to Allah, Allah the good, Allah the bountiful in whom
all men trust and who leaves the wheels of the world for men to turn! For
behold when they came down on the morning of the fourth day, even they
themselves did not understand what they had done. The body of Emir Sarif
Badian lay dead on the rooftop. Only then did the attendants understand how
indeed their bread, their palm oil and their water had been taken from them,
how their Emir had passed away.*

*At this time too Prince Ahmed and his wicked band knew that the
darkness, the wind and the rain had prophesied destruction on the house of
Emir Sarif Badian. For such was the will of Allah, may His name be praised!
Inscrutable his ways are for men to understand why the good suffer and the
evil prosper. But Allah knoweth best and in a moment of time he taketh away
the grain and the leaf. And Sarif Mohammed, no longer wayward, passed
into the arms of Allah, the Receiver. And his kingdom passed to a usurper."*

This is the song the griots sang, near an old red clay wall, near where the mule had implanted a fresh hoofmark and the obstinate ass had refused to pass. Near the feet, dusty feet, of children romping in dry sand, where the sea had come and gone milleniums ago. This was their song as three generations later Prince Ahmed the third lay dead in the palace.

*　　*　　*

Mohammed's wife, Queen Shade, had said that it was better to travel at night. Then there would be less chance of recognition.

"Why couldn't we stay?" the little boy asked her. He was only fourteen and he still felt that his doubts, his very refusal to believe, could explain away all that had happened. She was washing their clothes near a river and the Keeper of the Stables stood by her as he usually did.

"Your father was killed," she replied tersely, folding the clothes over and slapping them against the side of the bank. Legs tucked under her as she stooped, she quickly realized how impatient her reply was and she motioned to the Keeper of the Stables, "Why don't you tell him?"

"I, madam?" She nodded. Her eyes were on the distant hills.

The Keeper of the Stables looked at this slender woman with reeds in her hair, washing clothes by the side of a deep river as she frequently had to do on this journey and thought back on his mission. Emir Mohammed had told him, "If I do not come down from the housetop on the fourth day, you take Queen Shade and my son with you and go unto her kinsmen. There is nothing here except death; my mother Queen Abu hath died but soon, and my father hath long since passed away."

On that morning when Prince Ahmed came down alone from the rooftop with the third sign of Allah, the Keeper of the Stables saddled two horses in the courtyard and galloped away with Queen Shade. At first she had told him what to do, where to stop, how often to let her son, Yacub, rest. But as the grassland stretched out farther and farther ahead of them, and as she seemed farther and farther away from her home in these strange forests, she gave fewer frequent commands. He took over the reins more and more, especially as he was familiar with the countryside and recognized in what villages he would be most welcome, and in which wandering cattleman's shelter they could sleep.

As they traveled he got more and more used to her body's nearness, especially after they had buried her horse and had had to rely only on his. She was a slender woman with firm, tight muscles, a quick easy laugh as she turned

62

back sometimes to say something to him. They moved on, always at night as she had wished. And the journey was so long that the Keeper of the Stables thought he could almost see the boy grow before him, guarding his mother, being just a little more protective of her.

"Haven't we passed this stream before?" she asked suddenly one day. His reassurances were at first enough, but finally Queen Shade knew that she was a prisoner, locked on one saddle with a man who had been the Emir's Keeper of the Stables and with her child, Yacub. She decided to rely on her cunning, to say nothing as the landscape grew more and more monotonous, as they continued to circle it more and more. Soon he would have to make up his mind to do something. Meantime, she watched while pretending to sleep, for any chance of escape, unbeknown to him. She and this man were there, together, chained to an immovable horse with Yacub, her son.

It is this very woman that the Keeper of the Stables guarded on the morning when she stooped, knees out, to wash clothes. After she spoke he took the boy aside and spoke to him for some time. Then something happened which she had guarded against for a long time. It happened suddenly. He came back, munching a chewing stick, saying, "I sent Yacub to the village behind the hills which we passed half an hour ago. He will come back with food from my people." There was an insolent swagger in his walk.

Her heart skipped two beats and she watched his reflection in the stream as he walked up and down behind her. Then he too was gone, at least seemingly so and she turned round and all she felt was his weight that threw her back against the side of the stream and sent her newly washed clothes flying. His eyes were intent, but filled with a strange sorrow as he tugged at her wrapper.

"No," she tried to sound imperial. "Was I sent to *you* by your master? Or did he not urge you to take me to my father's palace?"

He grunted, as if he were an animal in great pain. He was strong and held her arms down with his left hand, and after tugging off her wrapper with his right, brought his right knee down and kicked open her legs. He saw the back of her head seemingly stretch out on the surface of the stream. "You are my queen," he cried out.

By now her protests were made mute by the positioning of his right hand which cupped her mouth. He did not work his way slowly in but jabbed frantically, silently, at her with the haste of spurs. And she shut her eyes in shame as she felt the water well up in her to ease his coming in.

On her now, he rode her gallantly as he would his horse. Her hair was dipped in river water but he did not notice; except now and then when he pulled frantically at strands that seemed to stand up all on their own like reins. "My queen," her rider repeated. Riding her with a passion and a fury, a wild connecting of skin and limb, a twist of bone, a tug of hair, towards some blind purpose. He saw his eyes wide open in the water, eyes which did not blink, across which a stained rim had seemed to pass like a bleeding cloud. She surrendered under the deft control of the Keeper of the Stables: He with the long whip and the deft hands was steering her through savannahs she had never known before. She bit frantically on his hand and tasted blood and her breath spluttered, coming in short stabs and gasps, as this male man galloped on her with all the grace and rhythm of an emperor. He who had been Keeper of the Stables now had his own mare, the riddle said, a wild dancing pony which coughed and shook him, up to the very sky, her short gasps coming quicker now, glazy eyes looking up to the still crown of his head, near her son's shoulder, near Yacub's shoulders, her son who hit him heavily with the limb of a tree.

His weight fell off her slowly and she felt the terrible wrench of his body away from hers, as the boy hit him again and again until all Yacub's fury was spent. Queen Shade cried out to her son, "You saw. He tried to rape me - he was raping me."

But the boy only turned away from her, threw the branch far out into the stream and started walking towards the hills.

"Wait," she cried. "Yacub! Wait for me! It's not as you think - " She struggled to retrieve her wrapper from the sand and stood up unsteadily to tie it round her. The boy was running now, "Yacub! Please!" she shouted again. But he had gone. His small frail body over the hill had disappeared beyond the trees. Near her the food the boy brought - bread, palm oil, water - the body of a silent man and the still impassive river.

\* \* \*

Had to hand it to them, Stephan thought. These African folk had some goddamn sense of something. Call it what you like. Back in Charleston a Black man was like any other Black man. You buried him, except you were from some crazy Gullah island and then you stayed up all night and did God knew what. Sarki pointed with a lean finger. They had walked in the sunset for about fifteen minutes. The cemetery was curiously quiet and there were few of the flowers or the crosses that he had been used to. As they had come in, he had said to Sarki, pointing to a nearby flower garden, "What the hell is that?"

64

"Europeans," Sarki had replied. "They look after their graves and tend the dead. There they rest quietly," Sarki concluded reverently.

Later on he struggled over tall grass and hoped to God that no objecting snake would dispatch him to the hospital. He asked Sarki, a trifle whimsically, "Your people obviously don't. This is like a wild field."

"Our people are not here."

"Then where the hell are you taking me?"

That was when Sarki pointed. "That's where my great-grandfather is buried. His body only. It does not matter. He is not there."

Yep, Mr. Sarki. Like Jesus Christ. Got up and sped away - on the third day? And where pray did he go?

"We believe they live with us," Sarki replied, almost reading his thoughts. The same shit, he said to himself. The same bull that Dele was forever talking about at home. The dead who were never truly dead. The dead who were under the ground but whom her boy-priest could evoke and speak to. He should have known. Crazy folk are crazy folk! You find them everywhere! The boy stood out in his white robes against the declining sun. "I wanted you to see your family," Sarki said simply. "These are your neighbors."

Stephan smiled as they walked back. He didn't give a damn. The road was going past here next month or the month after. Even if his grandfather was buried there. The bulldozers were coming in and the nice European cemetery with its flowers and neat rows of graves where the silent English lay in peace, all this was going to be turned up too and he would spread tar.

As they got back into the car, the boy said to him, "For us it does not matter. But I wanted you to see." Yes I have seen, m.f. I have seen some grass and a mound of earth and rocks and the darkness coming down. That's what I've seen.

"He was the Keeper of the Stables," Sarki explained as they drove away. "His son cared for the horses of Emir Mohammed, as he himself had done for Emir Sarif Badian."

Crazy words like the Black History teacher at Frost's place; she would have loved this. A real grave. She could have photographed it and sent it back to her friends in America.

"Let's go somewhere and have a drink. Graves tire me out," Stephan stated. Sarki smiled and they drove on the dirt road for a mile or so away from the cemetery. Outside there was only the absolute silence of the African nights, the occasional flash of a firefly.

"You know you remind me of someone I used to go with. Chick named

Dele. She would have dug all this."

And she would. Dele sitting up high in bed puffing at some joint and saying about how she was at peace with her world. That she did not feel cut off since everything was so near her. Dele fingering those damn beads which never came off and talking about her ancestors and some god whose name he could never pronounce nor scarcely remember now.

"You a priest?" he asked suddenly.

He saw the boy nod his head in the dark and Stephan came up at the same time to the tarred road.

"What kind of a priest?"

"I come from a family of stable-keepers. We were griots attached to the Emir's family and it was for us to remember the importance of history - "

"Never had much time for that myself," Stephan replied. "I prefer the present. Now," he pulled up outside. "My weakest subject."

Should have known better than to have walked in this goddamn place. Arranged like a circus. It seemed as if everybody, or at least most people knew Sarki. They were crowding round him. Then he suddenly saw the boys in white come out from behind an enclosure. They all fell down at Sarki's feet and Sarki motioned Stephan to sit. Like a man in a daze he complied.

"Your *oriki* - praises," Sarki stated shortly. "Did I ever tell you that you resemble a man from the South?"

"I want a drink," Stephan grumbled, wiping his forehead. It was damn hot. "Do you mean we're going to get some more history?"

Sarki said nothing. The boys in white rose and began chanting. One played on a small drum, another hit what looked like two pieces of steel together.

"A drink - "

"Moslem country," Sarki whispered. "Listen. Perhaps you will hear something."

He listened. They droned on and on in a monotonous wail. Why the hell did he always have to be exposed to history in this damn place?

"These are the griots," Sarki whispered. "The young priests in training you saw with me. They, like me, have inherited their tongues from their dead fathers. Or else," Sarki murmured above the racket, "every old man who dies would be a library that burns down." The small drum was beating alone and one of the boys was looking steadily at him, Stephan thought, and singing. Nearby there were some tables ranged round and he saw, of all people, Miss Cecily Dawn herself, drinking it all in. She must have given herself a project.

She nodded at him and he thought he saw the hint of a smile.

The boys were not grouped in their own circle and Sarki was leading them. He felt someone close to him and looked up.

"You don't understand, do you?" the earnest one said.

"I thought this was a bar," Stephan muttered crossly, "and I only came in for a drink."

Cecily Dawn laughed. He was actually glad to see her in the midst of all this. "Do you understand what the hell they're saying?" he inquired.

"Not all, but this much. They're tracing the lineage of Emir Sarif Badian."

"Oh? I've heard so much about that damn man that I feel we're blood relatives," Stephan exploded.

Sarki was chanting in a low voice, accompanied by the other priests. Cecily Dawn explained to him, "It's about how Queen Shade escaped and was raped." She listened carefully and then continued, "had another child when she went back to her home in the South. I can't get this part but it seems that she was raped - "

Oh God, he thought to himself. Here too. The effects of American porn creeping in! "One child had run away from her and she had another. I can't understand that bit. Oh Prince Yacub ran away. She had another child - "

"Cecily," he asked, "don't you ever stop? When do you start living for now?"

Her eyes were still fixed on Sarki. It was almost as if she had not heard him speak, "She spoke another language. They're saying that she was at one time the *iyawo* of Emir Mohammed - "

He touched her and whispered teasingly, "Don't you wish you had your tape recorder and your camera?"

Again the young priests prostrated to Sarki, kissing the ground with their lips. "Strange," she murmured, "they don't do that here. I wonder why?" They arose like a cloud from the dust and formed a semi-circle. Only the tiny drum was sounding now. They were like people in a trance. Then Sarki walked out and rejoined him and the young boys vanished suddenly.

"Did you understand?" Sarki asked.

"Sure, every word. You know how good I am with languages - "

Sarki smiled. "It was your *oriki*," he said crisply. "And mine too."

Cecily Dawn had gone again, probably getting autographs. "Sarki," he said humbly, but with a slight trace of irritation, "you know I don't understand a damn thing."

"Do you care?" Sarki's voice was insistent.

He shrugged his shoulders.

"Men are not born like parrots," Sarki commented. "Don't you wonder sometimes?"

His humility, momentarily there, had left Stephan as he answered, "I thought we'd gone over that already. Nigger grandfather came off ship in Charleston, called himself Hamilton. That's who I am. American nigger. Yassuh." Stephan saluted.

"Why don't you listen to those voices?" Sarki wondered.

"I don't understand what they say."

"The language?" Sarki speculated.

"Yep. The goddamn, motherfucking language. This here nigger talk only English." There was silence. Some of the people had started drifting out.

Cecily Dawn came over to him again saying, "I must leave now." She pointed to her charges, since seemingly she had brought some of them with her. In the background he saw her friend, the White Biology teacher, soaking up the atmosphere. Then they both disappeared.

"The Keeper of the Stables was my great-grandfather and the man whose grave I just showed you." Sarki reminded him. "He came back here and told the story of what he had done to Queen Shade. He was very ashamed to face his children here. He killed himself a day after he came back."

"How long ago was all this?" from Stephan.

"Three generations ago. But we still know their customs of prostration - "

"Do we have to talk about it now? Isn't there something we could do? For God's sake let's do anything. Grown men don't sit up all night listening to stories."

"Unless it's their story," Sarki shot back.

"Their story?"

The priest nodded. "My grandfather became the Keeper of the Stables. Our own priests feel that Queen Shade had a child - "

Stephan thought about this for a moment, not sure whether he ought to laugh.

"A beautiful ending," Stephan said. He applauded mockingly. "Something like television at home. Only no grime, brother, no muck - "

"What did you call me?" Sarki asked, looking at him intensely.

"Man that's just an expression Black folks use. My father used to say, every neighbor is my brother, is my sister. So you're a brother. And you're an African nigger. That helps." Stephan smiled.

"One day," the priest promised, "you will understand." He got up and

Stephan followed him outside like a lost person.

*　　*　　*

Prince Yacub sprinted down the hill and away from the river. Na shame they shame me today. I no know that so Olodumare go make me feel this way, Olodumare, the Highgod. Na so I find me own mother under the body of one nasty person who body smell of horse shit. Na this I born for? Today na true thing me be orphan. No father, that I know, and now no mother. Think I fool-fool. Think I no sabby what my own mother do when him let that man ride am like a horse, like my father him horse.

With the wind he ran and his mother's cries faded into the distance. All time maybe that's what me mother want, for that man to take am the way he take am, and ride am like a horse. That woman not know who he be? He no understand that he be queen, me be the son and today he put shame na me eye and expose himself to common person so. As the wind ran with him and the evening cooled, the prince heard himself rehearsing a psalm.

Suppose me nar sheep and Olodumare na the man who dey mind the sheep. I no go want nothing. He go bring me near better water where palm tree grow, he go help me with this *wahala* I face today. He go teach me fine fine thing so I no go do nothing wrong. Then all that thing what dey happen go turn back, and good thing go happen to me. And when I dead go, he go put me in another town and na there I go stay all time.

If I no believe now in Olodumare, na who I go think of? Never, never, all this time I feel so shame. Never, never in all this time, I feel so alone. The boy looked at the moving sky and the earth that seemed to run under his feet. Maybe he done dead. Maybe I kill am. But that not a wrong thing to do. If my father self know, he go thank me for what I do. For that man he not good. He no be the fine man I think say he was. Send me to buy food and then take my mother. My own mother!

Out of breath Prince Yacub stopped near a small clearing and sat down under an iroko tree. The large leaves felt cool, even though they were far above him and the enormous limbs of the tree curled at the side of his back. Which side I for run? Small pickin like me no know. But it no matter now. My house done fall down. My father he die, my mother shame me. Yes she shame me today. It no matter if I find meself back in Ahmed him power, for what thing he go do me? I no care and I no get feeling again. Everything done leave me when I see how dey fight so to make my father die and then drive my mother away for

69

one man to ride him like horse.

Prince Yacub fell asleep. But his head was still throbbing with what had happened to him. His feet were sore and one of his toes bled. In the distance the sounds of the night and a sky overcast. The Prince lay under the iroko tree, still, like a dead man, until the sun rose and was shining in his face. Hot. But it was no sun. Instead there were, it seemed to him, a hundred faces round him with flaming torches and the sky was bright now. The men closed slowly in.

Startled, he gave a cry, a shriek of terror and backed towards the tree. He fell against one of the heavy roots that had shoved its way out of the earth. The men closed in from all sides. At first he was going to try and break their line and run again. But it no matter? This shame is a small shame. Let them come catch me like animal, take me to the *oyinbo,* sell me. Make I go travel on another big water, on a floating hut, make I go. This Africa - what thing it give me? Me who been prince and who dey live in fine fine palace. Put collar round my foot, you hear. Tie me like horse. Make I run with all them other person who dey dey. Make I run fast. When I no run beat me. I know what thing you have to do. Na the fort we go go. You go lock me up and that big house go come and take me over the big water.

When he stumbled it was the first time that Prince Yacub had felt such pain. The whip whistled through the dark night air and landed on his back and his feet. "Up! Up," somebody yelled. And he started running again but this time his ankle was bound securely to the foot of another, his neck chained fast to the hand of the slave catcher.

I think, I no know, but the place which side I go they no go sabby me, I no go sabby them. Even the small talk I talk, this lillibit English I learn, they no go sabby. When I tell them make I go, what thing they go say. Yes, go, you na king son and queen son. Make you go back to your palace. We free you. We no want palaver. Na commoner we look for. Not king son. But it no go go so. Eshu, the trickster god, na him only know, na so they story no go go.

That place which side I dey come, it no get king nor queen. All person be the same. Them lay down in the night on the hard floor like servant, nobody to light fire near your bed, nobody to wake you for morning time, tell you say make we go out play with bird, catch fish. All men na the same. Thief man, priest man, old man, young boy. They catch all. Maybe death like this. But death no go be so hard. When person die, na another town he go to, so he can watch them other one who still living.

Yacub ran with his ankles fastened, driven by the men who had come deep into the interior to seek out slaves. Sometimes they rested near a stream and he turned his eyes away in shame when he remembered his mother and her hair in the water and the tall man with hard skin who rode on her body. And the slave catchers would duck his head in the water until he drank and beat him till he ate and when he saw his face clearly reflected in the glass of the water, Yacub knew that he had grown in three short days, had sprouted hair on his chin and that there was only a going forward.

Suddenly one morning there was the rank smell of that big river in which no man could see his face. In the distance the low sky came to meet it and he saw that the shoreline was wet with the same sand he had known at home. There was the tangy taste of salt in the air and just near him a moving house with large pieces of cloth tied round a pole. Yacub said to himself, Olodumare, make you forgive them. They no know what bad thing they do. But no answer came back and down in that dark hole of the fort he gave up his living ghost for the dead one that would take him seawards.

71

# CHAPTER 6

"I am not dead," I said.

Under the circumstances I thought I did fairly well, I distinctly remember the smell of green coconuts. The young boy, with army stripes across his face, slapped me again.

"You are dead," he insisted, adding with disdain, "Stephan or Grandman or whatever you call yourself!"

Now it is not often that this sort of thing happens to me. I consider myself a reasonable man. I have lived reasonably, ate more or less the right things, fornicated neither more nor less than anyone else. It was no use remonstrating. If they intended going through with this ridiculous charade, I felt I might as well remain quiet. And see what would happen.

"You are dead," this man said again. "You died last night at a quarter past three in the morning. It was all rather odd really. Because we were just leaving the village and then you appeared. They shot you by mistake." I was quiet. I am not a soldier. I do not engage in wars. I am no hot-blooded pacifist either. I do what I have to. There is no question usually in my mind about where my duty lies. I know. Instinctively. I have never sat down at a lunch counter or in a square. I prefer a chair. I did not reply.

"Come with me to the other room. There's a cocktail party there. He will talk to you."

The whole matter was a little absurd now. Who he was, I was supposed to know but in fact I didn't. Why (granted I was dead) they should choose to hold a cocktail party on this of all evenings I could not fathom. Again I refrained from speaking. I thought at some stage the terrible mistake would become apparent or that he would recognize me for whom I was. People have never wanted me for anything - I mean anything simple that is. My life is (and I insist on the *is*) sometimes a bore, rather exciting on weekends, rather sane. Sane

73

men are not wanted; hence my imprisonment.

I got up off the floor and followed the young man with the blood-stained shirt. Now I could see him a little better. He was certainly very young; very much the kind of person who ought not to be left alone with a gun. Much too young for guns, I would have said, if anybody had asked me. But in fact nobody did then. The next room was marked "For Use on Special Occasions." It was a large room and one wondered how so many people had gotten into it. The men and women and the few Mongols I saw were all very well dressed. I looked at my own crumpled clothing and wondered if I should say something, but reflected with a certain self-content that if I were supposed to be dead, then they could not really see me. And so it did not matter. In fact only the Mongols took the slightest notice of me.

They were all standing round in little groups. Sometimes they had glasses before their lips as if they were speaking but did not want to be observed. One or two were actually speaking, at least their mouths were moving but I could hear nothing. It was all really rather odd, so completely silent. As if this were not enough I saw in one corner of the room two colored gentlemen, a Chinese I believe and one of a darker complexion, doing what seemed to me like physical jerks and saying, "Ah! Yah! Ah! Yah!" just like that, over and over again. I noticed too, as I was moved fairly rapidly by my attendant through the room, that everybody possessed an empty glass and kept helping himself from a decanter on a long table, covered with an altar-cloth.

Then I found myself face to face with him. To describe this beauty is not easy; in a way he reminded me of Dele. He was tall and wore a large black gown. His fingers were the first thing I noticed - long and pointed; the nails, I observed with some satisfaction, must have been chipped from too much nail-biting and one finger was down to a stub. Immediately I started to sing, a long praise-song. I thought to myself as I did that it was rather unusual for me, at that time of the day or night, to begin singing not *to* myself but *at* somebody. I forget what I sang but I obviously did not upset him unduly for he merely inclined his head in my direction when I had finished on some grand note about how one is silent before the truly beautiful. Very corny, I now think on reflection but at the time it seemed just right. This was indeed the last direct statement I was allowed to make to him. After that he did most of the talking.

"Person," he stated. I almost laughed. I mean he was beautiful, but he took himself so seriously now. Did he not remember me? "You have been sentenced because of all you are." He paused. Someone wiped his forehead with a handkerchief.

"Person," (how I wished he would not call me that) "You have been found out. There are ten charges I have against you and I shall read them out before I sentence you to life." Again that pause. I looked at his toes. They were in sandals. Curled up beneath the leather. I could have said this or that about the past - his and mine that is. But I didn't. It wasn't important. The dream that I woke into kept coming back.

*     *     *

And in the evening I remembered my own past. I recalled the first spring of youth when the world was young and the yellow of the woodtrees that walked onto the edge of sea-shore was only stubble, and there were tracks before roads that anchored people at bay, wrecking their souls in the harvest of first hope. I had thought that youth would never pass, that it was all time, everywhere. I would never at that time have thought of myself as old, as an old man, about to die, hell-bent for my own funeral.

And when I gazed out and saw the purple hills lying like a package against the sky with the faded brown trees climbing down for safety, I thought that perhaps it was not so bad after all. I mean living. There was the day - it had different moods - at times quiet like judgement, at other times it made the noise of a hundred warriors killing rocks. The sea was big water, my people used to say, and so it was. It was. And the night came and went with the surf bathers.

*     *     *

The bell always went at four-thirty. At first it used to wake me and I would lie face upwards in the still dark until the light came on and I heard the noise of the others - the clatter of the chamber-pots, mattresses being hastily thumped, distant indistinct shouts. But now I woke the bell; I never knew when but every morning I woke at some still point of the dark when movement had ceased and not yet begun, before the humming had started. What I listened to in those tense still moments was simply an absence of sound - to absolutely nothing ringing in silence about my ears - and it was this that saw me through the next day and the day after to the accumulation of mornings that I had spent there.

I got up on this particular morning and fumbled round in the dark. They had been kind enough to give me a match - just one - and a box - with a lot of matches I might set fire to myself or to the place (which in their eyes was worse). But after all these mornings they had gotten used to me and my ways - they gave me a match every night before lights out. It was always the same face too that came to the grille - one day, I thought, by God I shall spit at him, I hate his face. And then I checked myself suddenly. Why? The man was only performing a kindness for no reason whatever. As the mornings added up, I myself ceased to matter, I thought, although - well perhaps in some way I did. At first there used to be a mention of my name on the radio of the discovery of the plot to overthrow the government they called it. But they didn't remember now. They were too busy building schools, I thought viciously. Damn them! And roads. And bringing back the foreigners.

When I found the match I grated it against the side of an old matchbox I always kept. At first nothing happened. The sulphur was wearing thin. I scratched again - a little bit in desperation. If the match should flicker and then go out I would have to lie for God knew how long in the dark, waiting for them and their infernal bell and the faint light above my bed to come on. With a frantic effort I got the match to light and the cell trembled into shape. The rough wooden chair, the mat in the corner, the steel bars. I thought grimly - how conventional! Why couldn't they think of a new line in cell-designs? Did they have to be as morbid as this?

That was the signal and it was only a few seconds later that I heard the padlock outside and the door creak open on its hinges. It was the same man - the one who gave me the match every night. He said, "Sir they're waiting." I only nodded. The man was officious. "My name is Per, Sir, short for person. I think you will remember me." It was not a question, it was a sort of whining statement. He did not answer as he tip-toed out and we closed the door behind the man, Per, ensuring that it was locked again.

"I think you remember the match, the light."

"Yes."

Per was satisfied. We walked easily along the corridors. The cell doors were lined up on both sides, their occupants fast asleep. When we passed fourteen, I remembered something.

"I want to go back," I said.

Per halted. "Back Sir?" I nodded. "But they are waiting. There is a car for you."

"I have forgotten something," I said shortly, as I would have done before. Per turned back and led the way. For a moment I became conscious of the fact that I had never really known Per - the whole of him that is. What I had seen every night was a disembodied face and a small withered hand proffering a match. That was all I knew. The "Sir" was as new as the servility was new. In the corridor Per quickened his steps saying agitatedly, "The bell will go soon, Sir. You have to be away by then. They are waiting in the pavillion."

"Who?" I asked.

"Oh, Sir. The people! The people!"

The way Per said it he made it almost sound as if they were alive and human.

"The people?" I asked.

Per looked back quickly at me. For a moment I resisted the impulse again to spit in his face. Who were these people? I thought. In my day they came when they were summoned and made noises of delight or sorrow as they were told. They fed themselves somehow - I did not know how. Some were poor, some rich. Some wore clothes and some begged. Who were these people? We reached the cell-door again. Per started fumbling with the padlock, hastily looking at his watch as he did so.

"They have never forgotten," he said. What could Per mean, I wondered?

"Ten years is a long time," I said. My cryptic style was coming back.

"The people are waiting, like me, sir. I have been waiting. I have been true to the party - you will tell them about the light, Sir, won't you. You will tell them about the light."

I went into the cell and sat on the chair. Per grew agitated.

"We must hurry, Sir," he said. "The bell will go in five minutes." I picked up the new matchbox and the match that he had discarded on the floor, I put the match into the box and said, "Yes I will tell them about the light." Per tried to grab at the box, to pull it away. "Souvenir," he begged softly. Per stood in the center of the room. I could barely make out his form.

"You can't take it," he bellowed. He was the warder again.

"Why not?" I asked simply. "You gave me."

Per tried to grab it. I put it in my pocket. I did not move, only continued sitting in the chair.

"Tell me about the people," I said as Per stared, "who are waiting in the pavillion."

Per, who had been standing near the door, left it and came across. "I am pleading with you and asking you, Sir, in the name of the party - "

"Tell me about the party, then," I asked pleasantly. Per grabbed me about my shoulders. I threw his hands off violently.

"You won't talk, eh Per? You won't talk. All right let me tell you. There have never been any people nor any party. At first there were the two of us only

- Ianty and me and we were everything."

Per said, "Sir the time - "

"And when the British left it was still the same - Ianty and Grandman. There were never any people. They did what they were told. And then the boys started coming back with degrees and no jobs. Discontent. Per, let me tell you about revolutions."

The bell rang, loud, short, penetrating. Per made for the door. I tripped Per up easily and he fell flat on his face. Then he got up and banged the door shut.

"Now you can't get out," I said. "You will have to sit and listen to me. And then they'll come and find you with the keys and me with the matchbox and they'll know what you were planning - I'll tell them everything. I've nothing to lose."

"It was all for the party, Sir," Per said, "I never believed in the others."

"Don't you understand what I say. There was never any party. There were men who came and voted and talked and made speeches to the radio. We made the decisions." Per tried to get up. "No you don't," I threatened. "I am not going to give you the chance you wanted for such a long time - the chance to see me dead."

"Dead, Sir?"

"Yes, dead. Do you think I am more than a little stupid? Do you think that I didn't know that those matchboxes were soaked in gas? That you hoped - for ten years Per that one morning you would come and find that I had lit the box too near to me and scorched my face or blinded my eyes. The rest would be easy. You could then burn me and the bedclothes and run yelling fire." Per tried to get up again, but I motioned him with my feet. "Get up and I'll kill you. I have every reason. You have no right in my cell. You're not even on duty." He relaxed again.

"Why don't you say something, Per? Say it was the party. I know it was the great Two-for-Three. Those were his orders. Get rid of him and you were going to carry them out. I was to be catastrophe number 25/6 - a number in a file. I wonder if I would have merited mention in the local news."

I could now hear the sounds of activity in the other cells. Someone was whistling. Someone called out: "Bo how de body?" And hearing no reply, he said, "How, Doc?" I went to the cell wall and yelled, "I O.K. brother." That was a friend. For the last ten years he had called out every morning. Just like that. He didn't know who I was and I suspect that if he knew he wouldn't have greatly cared.

"That's the people for you Per. I've never seen him but I feel I know him. I have seen you and I know I hate you."

I went across to Per and Per turned up his face. I spat straight at him. Per leapt up and went towards me and I let him come. I knew that, though older, he was stronger; I could see now - it was getting brighter. When Per came I caught him in the crook of my right elbow and Per pummelled on my chest. I brought his hand right round.

"I am going to kill you," I said. Per fought even harder. He inched his way slowly to the door. Per had got his nails in my bowels and was digging at me for all he was worth. I felt the burning, smarting pain of fresh salt blood under his shirt. With a deft wiry movement Per freed himself and started for the door. Two steps and he would have been through, were it open. Per pulled up suddenly at the thought of what had happened. He was trapped. He stared at the door for a full few seconds. Then he turned round. He picked up his keys and stuck them in the spaces between his right hand fingers.

"You deceitful old idiot," he panted. I laughed and waited. Per circled round me. "I'll kill you," he shouted. "Execution of my duties. You were trying to escape."

I still laughed softly. I waited. He started talking again.

"It's too late now for that. The people in the square don't want me Per. It pleases him now to release me to show his magnanimity. When I come out, it is not me at all coming out of prison, it is he who is releasing me. The glory is his. And then I get pensioned off to somewhere nice with a rat like you for company who will probably poison me off."

Per continued circling; I could see him clearly now. The light was brighter and morning had come. The edges of the keys glinted in Per's hands. I continued speaking but Per was not listening.

"Let them wait. They have waited ten years. They can wait another twenty. Do you know," I spoke as if to myself, "that people are voting now who were only a mound of stomach when I came in and the boys of twenty-one at that time may well be young grandfathers." I laughed and Per came at me. I did not resist. I let him hit me hard with the point of the keys; they punctured my temple and blood started to run from my mouth. Per threw me on to the ground and then jumped over me. He started to stab at me viciously like a man gone mad, at my throat, at my bowels, anywhere, creating a fierce embroidery of terror. Then suddenly the cell-door was flung open and two guards and about four other people rushed in and separated us. Per stood against the wall and I sat there. A short man, youngish, with a blue suit on, said, "Detain that man," pointing to Per. He came up to me and stretched out his hand.

"The revolution is complete, Sir. We have won. The guards killed him this morning."

"The two of us - at first there were only the two of us - him and me and we were everything," I muttered, not thinking of either Ianty or Two-for-Three. The man in the blue suit said to some people who had appeared, "Hoist him up high and take him outside. Let the people see him."

They lifted me up. The last I saw was Per slumped against the wall, his fist tightly clenched over the keys, stabbing at the matchbox which must have fallen out of my pocket. Per was crying. I felt the blood pouring down me. Someone wanted to wipe it, but the man in the blue suit said, "No let his people see him like that." They bore me off shouting, "Grandman! Grandman!" At the prison-gates I saw the crowd. How big had all the children grown! They were yelling and screaming. The morning sun was already a little hot. Mounted police were keeping back the crowds. I looked round; they were all so young. There was not a single face that could have been over forty; they did not know me and could not know me. I saw one of the new skyscraper buildings out of the corner of my eyes - the signs of progress of the late party. Even the goats and the cock that crowed just near me on a fence were new. I saw faces looking up at me, twisted, turned, revolving around the sound of noise. And then I must have fainted.

# CHAPTER 7

Dele took a rosary out of a purse and gazed at it for a minute or two. Then she replaced it. She closed her eyes and her lips moved as if she were rehearsing a game she had learnt in childhood. Over her shoulders and face the early evening fell like a stole. Soon darkness would come over that like a nun's veil -and after that anything could happen.

There was only one window in the room which had a bed, two easy chairs, a chest of drawers, table and a wash-basin. Through the window she could see the sky made up for the awful finale of sunset. Pink cheeks and the sun like the red lips of a young girl and the darkness fingering the edge of sky, feeling the knees of the horizon. She went over to the wash-basin and washed her face. The loudspeakers started up:

> *From a hole to a hole*
> *That is life.*

She smiled a little and dried her face in a towel. Someone rapped on the door. It was a young boy with food. She looked from behind the towel.

"Make you put it there, please."

He put it down. She looked at him kindly.

"You go pay now?" he asked her.

"No. Tomorrow. Manager know."

He turned to go. She asked him, "Where you from?" He seemed embarrassed talking to one of the "lodgers." She bent down stroking his face.

"Are you coming tonight?" he asked.

She shook her head.

"The Prime Minister's coming with his wife," he said eagerly.

"I know," she answered. "That's why I'm here."

81

He turned to go. Outside the yard had grown more noisy. When the boy opened the door to go, she could hear the loudspeakers bawling and conversation like a whisper. She went through the door and from the verandah that ran round she had a good view of everything below. Behind the door the ladies were putting the finishing touches to their make-up and their conversation could be heard when a record was changed. The Manager was collecting his rent; those who could not pay in cash paid in kind. A few tables and chairs were occupied by people who were drinking and eating chicken. She thought to herself how much the scene seemed to be set for a murder, for violence, for sudden death and action - any action to end these years of confinement. She went back inside; the night followed her like a shadow and the music rushed back out when she turned on the light and closed the door. She started undressing, looking at herself in the mirror, remembering . . .

*     *     *

Suntime every morning Cousin Cordelia is waking up children. She has a large stick and with one movement of hand bring it down on the backside of her three pickin sleeping on the floor of the parlour. "It's crap-time, you hear?" she shout. "All must rise and shine." The oldest of the three jump up suddenly and, as he is doing every morning, he make his morning water over the bodies of the other two. Cousin Cordelia knocked the flow of his urine with sharp crack of stick and cursewords, "Nasty little bastard. Since your father dead and gone, I ain't have nobody, yah? Nobody. And every day you pissing over the other children." The boy screeching but persevering.

Finally the rest of the house coming out of nightness. Mr. and Mrs. Johnson hear their child screaming between them; Mr. Johnson swear, turn over and his wife hawk loudly and try to spit through the closed-up window. In the next room, where Dele sleeping crosswise on a bed, pack between the two children of her grandmother boyfriend, the parson, there is one big palaver as the two children fighting for space. Then Dele with a gentle movement kick one to hell off the bed and as he began howling she close her eyes, pretend to sleep and wait.

Then her grandmother, Mamma Smythe, begin. Since Dele return home with a belly, her grandmother left the house, claiming "I will not sleep with a bastard pregnant for another bastard." Morning time was when her grandmother return from the parson house and begin going through all the hymns in the hymn book. Then when the clatter come of child on floor, Dele hear her say, "No place in me own house. Daughter married, come back. Son married can't go. Grandaughter pregnant with bastard pickin."

On her first dry morning back Dele feeling the staleness of things. She had been left on a victorious evening and the street was like a dazzle. It was then rainy time, scorch season gone for good. She was loving. Stephan was from another country. "He is not from here, yah," she said to her friends. "Native man is no good. Only to poke you till your thing is sore and then they marry gentry lady who sabby book. They can curse my ass, say I am loving with foreigner. I don't care one shit. Foreigner get the same thing what is swelling just like native man. Foreigner treat me better. They open taxi door for me, stand up when I come into room. Native man is no good." And so she been gone.

Her grandmother say, "Girl, you going? And your ass will come right back here."

Dele laughed. Stephan living in a house high on a hill, in the bush, outside the town.

"Not all this talk-talk there," she reply to her grandmother. "Not all this niggergram. Nobody there where he is staying but bush-people. They are drinking their *amole*; when they are drunk they sleep and sex themselves." The man had laugh from the house next door and she shout at him, "Mind your own business, you anti-man. Watch your wife and she motor-car man. No mind me and my man." She was proud then.

Love is beautiful thing, she had thought, in the rain season when the water drizzle on her one night and she shelter with Stephan under a tree. She different with him.

"I frighten," she had said to Stephan.

"Don't frighten, girl. You people always frighten darkness. Nothing to frighten." He could even talk like them.

She look at him then. He only a small, young boy, really, like darkness out of which he talking like a father man.

"People in San Francisco don't frighten for everything like you people here."

"You go there Stephan?"

He laughed softly in the dark and hold her closer. He say nothing, for small time. Then he mutter softly. "And New York and London and Rome and Athens."

My God, she thinking, come this Sunday is straight in church I will take my ass. I will pray. Thank God for borning this mortal man. The man is not like blackman. The man is blackman and yet the man is not like blackman.

"Of course," Mamma Smythe been said when Dele first meet up with Stephan. "Is that what sweeten your frontside thing. He is a Johnbull. That's all. A Johnbull with Black man balls." Mrs. Johnson laugh. She herself had belly then. "Lawd have mercy," she say, "Johnson, you funny like rass-hole t'day. Is that that sweeten her. No mind her. Stranger-man will leave. Rainy season marriage always drizzle and stop."

Stephan come at the tail-end of her days. It was just, on looking back, as if she about to find herself completely in the chamber pot, with Mr. Thompson's ass over her. Twenty-one years and no man. Twenty-one years and no work. The only man you finding is married man. They poke you, one night, two night; they wash their *botu* in the sea and go home to them wife, smelling of salt water. No more married man now. There had already been too too many. Dele always used to say: I ain't blaming nobody. Is here they raise me up on my cross. Is here I must stay and suffer. Coup or coup on top coup don't make no difference to me. Whether the Prime Minister in jail and they fire pepper up his backside or they send him with his big belly back to State House; whether the military man is Major, General, or Captain Balls, it don't make no difference to me.

I have to look straight at every morning. Nothing to do. I have to walk till I get sore foot, looking a work. One time this lawyer give me a work and then he want to begin play with my bubby. Another time a Lebanese. They better. They don't play with you. They want to curse you and tell you how you is bush and you not fit anything. Is times like this she remember her father, with his large Mercedes, his fat mistresses, his house, his son, his wife. Just a piece of land, she always saying, a small piece of land is all I want, and two stone where I could live. He never do anything for me. Only come to town once every purple moon and hab my mother. Another time to buy me eat at the Paradise Hotel. "Is one eat I need? What of all the other eat-time I never get?" Her father laugh. And went back up-country to his bush-woman. They make money there. Diamond area. I never see one pauper cent.

If Stephan was not god almighty, who was god, she used to ask herself? He treating me like I is a person. No beating. But he know to jealous and like too too much palaver. Perhaps god is like that. End of month - you want dress, shoe, hat? What you like? At first she took his givings; then they no matter again. One end-month she say, "I don't want anything." And he look at her strangely, saying nothing first, then later, "Girl, is now you acting like Johnbull woman. Those kind of *titi* don't want anything from a man. Nothing." She had felt pleased. "You put your *tolole* in those white women *toto*?" she had asked unbelievingly. He had laughed. Only later she knew why when he told her of another girl named Dele in his own country.

*    *    *

Someone had said that somebody else had said that someone had said. Quite definitely the rumor began in Kissy, near the dockyard, made its way slowly up Westmoreland Street, through Pademba Road and by night-time it had paused at the Brookfields Hotel. There it was slightly altered and put on its way towards Spur Road and Wilberforce where the tied-to-their collar gentry dwelt. Cousin Cordelia had heard it near Padema Road near the lock-up where that jackass Grandman was. Someone had said:

"Mail boat never come yet - no onions."

Cousin Cordelia shrugged her left shoulder and continued walking. She looked at the lock-up where above the large steel fence there were live electric wires to prevent prisoners from escaping.

"Dele pregnant," someone else said. A man with a bowler hat asked Cousin Cordelia for a shilling. Cousin Cordelia stopped arguing with the boy from whom she was buying a trinket to abuse the man. "Dele pregnant?" she asked feigning disinterestedness. It would not do to let the person know that they were related.

"Dele pregnant."

"For a man?" another person asked as she stopped under a tamarind tree.

"For a man," the informant replied firmly and with conviction.

At first as she walked away, Cousin Cordelia felt fear and pride and regret. Dele had a belly. Someone was sticking his thing up her rass and she had thought all the time that she was dealing with a schoolgirl. Schoolgirl my ass! But rain make goat and sheep shelter under the same cellar. The same thing had happened to her and to Dele's mother and would happen to the bitch that Dele was making for some hot man. And so it would go on and on. As she walked home and her feet felt the burn of the pavement, she thought about herself and Dele. She really had never known her growing up. Dele had somehow got dumped in the house and left to fend for herself. Mamma Smythe was too old to be a mother and Cousin Cordelia had hoped that some day a fresh boy would come and see Dele and she would arrange the 'gaging. Then, she used to feel, she would talk to Dele and tell her to keep the man waiting - perhaps a year. She must not sex with him and when the time came for the

85

'gaging Cousin Cordelia would herself take the menstruation cloth for blessing to the priest and prepare rice bread.

It was as if all round her she could hear the laughter as she walked up Pademba Road past the houses with glass shutters and wooden windows that belonged to another land and then to Cotton Tree. Perhaps it was her imagination. A small girl who had been seeing her flower regularly and whose *toto* had never been pushed at by the *tolole* of mortal man could bear needle and thread, kola nut and alligator pepper from the boy's home. Cousin Cordelia used to see herself dancing on the way; "Yawo mami eby so" which was their way of saying that Dele had grown up and was as important as Cousin Cordelia.

Up Saunders Street where the cars hurl themselves at you and you could hear the shouts of the rowdy Kroos from the nearby market. One no-good loose boy leaned out of a window and shouted across the street; she thought of how the procession would arrive at the house. Then there would be the knocking and the boy's relatives would say they had come to find someone - a rose. She would show them all the girls present until they picked out Dele and knew her for what she was. But it was not to be, she thought sadly as she turned into her street, it was not to be. No Bible and ring would be given, no ginger-beer, no parson, no dowry, no 'gaging. Dele pregnant. Shame draw her into the house and she bolted the door. Let them laugh. Dele pregnant. Her belly swell round. Perhaps with a mortal man. Dele was no *akriboto* woman; she could sex and have children. To hell with the ginger-beer and the parson man.

Months later Dele walked the same road and a neighbor called out, "I give you joy." And the joy that was in her bowels moved and turned a little and she felt the first warm flush of a maker. If only it could be a *bobo*, a male-child, then the laughter would stop and the joy that people gave her with their lips would be in their hearts too. She knew that she was no *rary-girl* and it was not just Saturday night tea that caused it. Whether the father-man was Stephan, Ianty or the young doctor Pietro just back, did not matter greatly. What mattered more was that it should be man-kind like all of them.

"Don't walk at night without a stone in your hand," Mamma Smythe had cautioned. "Don't eat plantain or pineapple," from Cousin Cordelia. "Don't chop pounded food," from the anti-man next door who should know, since his wife had all those children he called "me pickin" from her motor-car man. "I give you joy," from all.

And she felt joy bursting out at her nipples and her breasts. Joy at her hips and in her bowels. Joy within. It had to be a boy-pickin and he would come and show them all that his mammy was gentry and he would be the fourth generation that had come to save them all from the starvation in their guts from waiting too long on mail-boats and the dryness of rain and the real hunger of those born without soil. For she had no delusions; this was the emptiest corner of the world where every man barricaded himself behind the walls of his family and even the 'famble' did not matter. Where bring-me-eat and sex-me were all that mattered and, if in a life-time a man built four crumbling walls to hide shame, he was a copper millionaire in dust.

*　　*　　*

"Dele?"

"Come in."

Sir Ianty went in. He was like a schoolboy. He saw Dele in bed taking off her shoes.

"Dele what have you come here for? To disgrace me?"

She said, "Hello Sir Ianty Pakeman."

He sat down heavily.

"I thought you had left the country," he said.

"Why?"

"Well after everything . . . "

"It didn't end for me then," she said. She looked him over carefully. "What a big boy you are - the great P.M. of Iota!"

He said, "Dele, what do you want? The governor is here, everybody. We are celebrating Independence night. Another year and we will be completely free."

"I don't care about your political rubbish," Dele replied, "I want to go away."

He got up and came across to her.

"Stay here and help me."

"You don't need me. A hundred women will follow you now."

"But you know me."

She got up and turned on the electric fan.

"Yes I know you. I know you for the selfish person you always were. Fourteen years ago I lived with you and you were selfish then. Now your selfishness is only bigger. Instead of just me you want all Iota."

"And I will get it," he replied. "It's not as simple as you put it. Politics is a business like anything else; we are in it for what we can get. Grandman was."

"What of the people out there who believe your Latinisms and your pomposity?"

"Well I don't care about the people. I could care about me and you."

"In that order," she replied. "What of the splendid White woman who decorates your household? What of her?"

"She is my wife," he said simply. "She is a good woman."

"She is your status symbol," Dele jeered, "the proof that you have arrived."

He came near her, clawing at her breasts. He was breathing heavily.

"Dele *you* left me."

"Yes I left you."

"For another man, for Stephan."

"Yes for another man. For Grandman. He gave me holiness and love. You gave me housekeeping money and sex."

"You were nothing but a whore. I could have made something more of you."

She pushed his hands vigorously off her. "Something? Something like what? We didn't want the same things."

"What do you want?"

"Love," she said simply. He smiled.

"You can have money from me now that Grandman, poor fellow, cannot help you. I'll put you in a house, you shall have - "

"The world each time I open my legs and I would die of shame. No. I don't want that. I want - " She broke off and continued, "Sunday is ill."

"Oh Sunday!" A pause. "Is he my child?" Another pause. "Sunday? I want to have him." She did not answer.

"Well you know my terms." He got up to go. "Come out and tell me when you know whose child he is."

As he turned the handle of the door she hurled herself at him and choked his neck.

"Prime Minister - hell!" she bellowed. "You are a stinking dirty man." He tried to grab hold of her but she was too quick for him. She bit him on his neck, screaming all the time. "How I hate you!"

A knock sounded at the door. The Manager came in quickly. But Dele had finished. The Prime Minister stood there breathing heavily, his shirt torn,

\u029free scratches across his face. The Manager said, "The police Sah! The police - these woman - "

Dele threw herself over the bed. The Prime Minister said nothing. He started walking out.

"You'll be sorry," Dele called out. When she put her nose on the mattress her shoulders shook, and silence soon came, thrown out from between her elbows.

*        *        *

Dr. Pietro did not know how long he drove; one street was very much like another, suddenly starting from the main road and ending at the cemetery, where they buried people and rubbish. The streets had no names except nondescript ones like A line, B line and so on. He did not remember Sunday now; a new excitement had possessed him, taken complete control and left him slightly nervous. He knew which line he wanted and he knew the routine; he would have to hide his car in the dark, at the back of the cemetery and walk over the graves. Then he was sure to encounter no one. And then when he came to the street he would see them - standing there in the three-quarter dark, sitting in front of their doors, their legs slightly open or lying on grass-mats. You chose a grass-mat and you lay down beside anyone and she opened one eye and gave you the secret of her thighs. In the morning you would pay.

That was why he liked new women because new women's thighs were always round and there was the mystery of sweat in the curvatures behind their kneecaps. New women were virgins, unexplored and adjustable. They smelt like fish after rain and tasted like cheese and olives. Wet and burning they fought fiercely, from the spring-joint of their thighs to their agitated nipples. And when they were greased and ready, groaning and panting, he hit them - hard. On their fresh, twisted mouths and he felt the sweet, hard rush of pain on his burning palms, the easy power of triumph over clean flesh moving beneath him.

Then new women cried and pushed at him begged for the mercy of God and the help of the devil when their ears tasted salt, when he had tasted blood from the bulge of their sweating cheeks. Then he connected with them and in this joining their fronts maneuvred together. Moving deeply in, he ransacked their bowels for the beyondness of pleasures and felt bone on bone, muscle on muscle, connecting.

Always he lived through this immediate darkness and sweat. She did not answer him at first.

"What for you, so 'fraid?" the cripple asked him.

"I'm not afraid," he said sharply.

She laughed, a hollow rattling sound.

"Why you always come by the cemetery?"

He started again.

"What do you know about me? Eh?"

He was afraid. She answered his question directly.

"I know you are the Italian doctor in charge of the hospital and that you came here from America. I live in hospital. I came from nowhere."

He stooped down and took her shoulders.

"Not so loud," he hissed.

"No soul here," she said, "only us."

"What do you want?"

"Few years ago no man go ask me that. He just take it."

His hands left her shoulders, repelled. He started getting up. "I be a woman," she continued. He saw the slippers she had on her hands, and the old car tires that protected her knees as she crawled. She clawed at him with one hand. He got up quickly and retreated two paces. She went after him, kissing his shoes.

"Dr. Pietro. Use me! Use me for five minutes."

He saw the headlights of a car in the distance and wondered for a moment what he should do. She held on to his shoes crying softly.

"I did know you since you used Dele."

The name was like a bell in his ears.

"Dele? Dele? What do you know of Dele?"

She made a sound, half-sob, half-laughter. Then he kicked her, hard with his right foot. She fell back sprawling, her mouth bleeding. She was not crying any more. He ran down the street quickly. Later, she would spit the blood and dirt out of her mouth and crawl back to the hospital.

\*　　　\*　　　\*

Quick night always comes early over the town, enveloping traffic in thin darkness. People get up from in front of their street-doors and go inside because spirits like to pass through open doorways at night. Night discolors every lamp-post and stains the street and stones grey, muffling every sound of the pacing world. Into every street in the world night comes in the same way, like a cover, over wrecked lives that lie in gutters, crowding with goats, lending terror and mystery to living. It is sure as eternity, as memories, when the intestines of the world come to the surface like stars and the grave cold moon probes the sky.

In the early cold night Dr. Pietro slightly scraped his trousers as he went over a fence. Then he smelt human excreta - it must have been an open sewer pit. Four pigs browsed around with sucking enjoyable noises. Someone emptied the remains of the day's cooking and a little splashed on his shirt. An alley cat crouched against a wall and two trees, mouldy and withered, grew out of excreta and ground. One more wall and then he would be there. He could hear the heavy boots of some army sentry doing an elaborate march with hard businesslike roundabout turns. He knew the man would not hesitate to shoot him - he would be carrying out orders - curfew at six and nobody at anytime allowed on the Paradise compound. He had to see Dele - he wanted to ask her a question which would make a difference to him. He crouched with the cat near the stone wall and when the footsteps of the guard faded away, he scaled the wall. Pieces of broken bottle at the top scraped his hands and made them bleed. He heard the guard's footsteps returning so he ran under a table in the adjacent dining room, wiping his bloody hands with his handkerchief.

He had to wait until the guard's face was turned to the stone wall and then bolt past the rooms where love was sold at five dollars a turn, through the doors and up the stairs. Dele would be in Number One. He heard the guard's feet marking time as he got ready to turn back and he bolted from under the table through the door and up the stairs. In the darkness he could not see so he sent a bucket of water clattering in some uncertain direction. "Stop," the guard roared in the darkness, returning quickly. He rushed into the yard and started looking frenziedly around. Dr. Pietro tapped softly on the window of Number One. No answer. Could it be that she was not there? He tapped again. Someone peeped through the curtain out into the darkness and he was snatched inside, as the guard came upstairs. He could not see for a long time as the room was pitch dark. "Dele," he cried out.

No answer. Was he safe? The guard's footsteps seemed to pause near Number One and then they continued downstairs. Dr. Pietro looked round him and saw Dele lying under a blanket.

"Dele," he said quietly and went to her bed.

In the darkness she rubbed his head on her breast. Suddenly, inexplicably he started crying. She smoothed back his hair saying nothing.

"I came," he began.

"Yes, I know why you came," she replied. Then she sat up and her breasts hung over the blanket, brown and bulging. She said: "Christ came back

too. All men are odd. I left you once and now you risk getting killed to see me."
She dried his eyes with her hands and he looked at her steadily for a long time.

"Tell me," he said, "what I want to know."

She turned her face away.

"You know about us. You should know."

"But I wasn't always impotent Dele. There was one time when Stephan left."

She looked back at him fiercely; her breasts erected themselves high against the blanket.

"There were several times," then softer, "but you were right - there was just once."

Dr. Pietro's voice seemed to be coming from far away from the darkness of the window.

"Dele, it matters to me more than ever now that Sunday should be my child. All my life I have wanted, not just things, I have had an urge which was never satisfied. As I grew older I realized how it came about."

Dele turned back towards him: "I don't want your life-story."

Dr. Pietro did not hear her. He continued: "I grew up in the back streets of Naples. I never knew a father. My mother sent me to school, kept the house during the day; at nights she went out. As I got older I understood and I took it for something as normal as the fried fish people sell, or the cheap trinkets they fool tourists with in the street. I grew up like any child; we went for outings to Sorrento and came back full of grapejuice and sea-water." In the darkness he laughed.

"Why are you saying these things. They hurt you, surely?"

"Not anymore. At thirteen, I tasted love. There was a dark-haired boy, of golden beauty and his bones were large. One day he touched my knees and everything in the region of my groin sprang to life. For the first time then I began to know a little bit of whatever love is, for my mother gave me a home and a school. Love, she kept for sale. Yes for customers. There was none left next morning." Dr. Pietro was breathing heavily now.

"What I want to say is that this dark-haired boy used to let me lie on top of him, or squeeze my legs together as I clawed at his knees and there was a whole new tingling feeling between my legs. That's part of what I wanted from you, Dele," he ended.

"That's satisfied me," she replied. "We were three years together and you took me with you as far as I could go. I knew I would leave because there was somewhere further up where you had built a tower of pleasure. No woman could follow you."

He put his hand delicately around her shoulders.

"I have always desired what we could not afford. After a while I could only take part of what I wanted. Is that silly? I don't know."

"At least you have a profession."

"But Dele even that I never wanted. I never wanted to amputate legs and cut off arms; so much of a doctor's life is destroying. I wanted to build, to save souls."

She laughed a little.

"I can't imagine you as a priest."

They heard footsteps outside passing up and down; it was the sentry doing his duty in this fatal way of Iota.

"No, not a priest," he continued, "perhaps just a praise-singer because I fell in love with the virgin god. I wanted to give birth to god-in-love. I am not talking of adoration. I am telling you of holiness - something that stabs at your heart with wonder and awe, fills your groins with power and pain. I hung her by my bedside long after the dark-haired boy had gone and in my wet dreams of loneliness I swear she came between my legs and taught me truth. It is to her that I sang."

"I don't understand all you say," Dele began.

"Let me tell you. I must tell you how important it is for me to have Sunday. As I said my mother died. I was seventeen, perhaps eighteen. I don't want you to feel sorry for me. She had left almost enough to see me through university. I stayed with a priest for sometime in exchange for nightly favors given between the father and the son and the holy ghost peeping at us. I was not sure what the priest was doing: certainly I never thought it was wrong. My virgin approved of it, for through it somehow I could come to her; all of her is holiness and from the incest of her kiss I got the water of life." Dr. Pietro stopped. In the darkness, only the silence hummed, making a sound like wind blowing over the edge of the world, coming from the lips of God.

"I understand not so much more now. Why did you leave Italy?" Dele asked.

Dele was halfway out of the bed now and the doctor hung his face down between her knees. He spoke looking up at her:

"I had to leave because once I had a climax, the virgin had gone. For three years she had sat over my head and crawled up between my legs. For three years I had stood and she had knelt to me and God's finger was always on my penis, telling me she must be virgin forever. Until that night the floodwaters of my system opened, I had my fill, and have never been a saint since then."

93

There was silence, then Dele asked slowly: "And what can Sunday do?"

"If Sunday is my child, he's pure; through him I can find grace."

Dele got out of the bed, the blanket around her. "Dr. Pietro get out of here. You are insane. Shall I give you my son for you to take him every night near his waist?"

"Is that all you understood tonight?" he asked quietly.

"Get out," she repeated, "or I shall call the guard. This is another time. You are a vile old man."

He said, almost as if to himself, perhaps to another: "Dele," touching the blanket. That was all. He went into the darkness outside and the early dawn coming down the stairs. It was a quiet morning, still a bit stale; the cobwebs of the night had not yet been cleaned away. In her room Dele sat up in bed listening to the crack of the ceiling. She was waiting. Then a shot crashed through the earliness of still dawn. She jumped back in her bed and pulled the blankets over her ears.

Then she got up and ran outside. Dele ran clickety-clack, click-click on the points of high heels, little holes in the soil, stiff road pressing against the tip-tap of calf-leather and steel point. The night grew round and she panted at it. The girl, running clickety-clack, pin-pricked at the silence and a watchman heard her and turned over, the booze singing in his dreams and a small boy named Sunday heard her and dreamt a wet dream of girls that came quickly and a drunk almost heard her except that he dozed flat out in bad breath and vomit. The street was half-lit by a blue lamp-light that swerved in part from the roof of the station hotel. When she swung into the narrow street with the railway station and the blue lamp, she dived suddenly into a corner and the hump of house-shadow covered her except that a tip of shoe-toe, white shoe-toe that leapt over rock-road, showed. It was easy for the car to see her, to spot-light her huddled back against the white wall of building. The car came slowly down the street and for a moment the girl's face moved. This time the watchman jumped at the sound and the boy, dried out of his dream, woke at a window and peered out at light and shadow. The huddle of light came at the dark wall and shattered it.

In the soft quiet night Dele could hear the footsteps of the world squelching near her as she walked. In the dark distance there was a shadow of light and she wondered if all revolutions began and ended like this.

"Stop!"

It jolted her and suddenly she became aware of faces pressing against hers and sweat and the long needle points of bayonets as the soldiers jumped out. They looked at her.

"Am I - am I - going the wrong way?"

There was no answer and the faces, some scarred, some gaunt, all greasy looked searchingly, and yet without expression at her. Something made her run before the soldiers caught up with her at the end of an alleyway. She did not struggle much.

* * *

And this was the first evening of the first day. And Grandman, proudman, walked the streets at curfew time. In prison he had gotten used to seeing everything at eye-level but now he could see the tips of tree-tops and the way that the thunderless lightning arched the sky-line, shimmering sky and leaf-fringe. It was god-night and this, my city, had never loved me, but in spite of everything I have always worshipped it for it was beautiful and naked. After trudging up Wilkinson Road where he was a boy scratching his foot on the dry road, he came to Congo Cross.

He almost laughed loudly. So this was the blessing that the last government had bestowed on a hungry populace - a fountain! The water leapt erratically into the air and he remembered the thirsty villages up-country where at this very hour the children would be reciting endless *suras*. Up hill, past the new houses for the new rich and he came to Wilberforce. There you could look down at my city, he thought, and adore it. Every light was a sacrament and all round the sea coveted the land. He almost prayed a thanks to life.

Three soldiers suddenly rushed at him out of the darkness. He stood his ground and said with some of the old firmness, "Down." They prostrated when they recognized him. He left them lying on the road and continued walking. Perhaps he could ride on a *poda-poda* and go the Regent, his village where he was born. Perhaps he would meet Dele there.

When he got on to one, it was just like before. A man had his elbow in Grandman's face and a woman's smelly basket of fish accentuated the purpose of her journey. An old pa with nothing better to do, said to him: "Better days done come."

"Na why you feel so?" He had not been recognized in the darkness.

"Dem old wicked government done gone. We go have another one. Grandman free."

The old man did not stay long. The conductor, a small boy who kept

95

saying to the driver, "Le' we go," told the old man he had to get off if he was not going to pay an extra fare. Grandman thought to himself. Did they like palaver as much as the old days? Ten years is a long time. Grandman said provokingly: "Na so you go talk to the man. He fit to be your father."

"Me sah?" the boy laughed. "I get better father pass this one. Me daddy fit pay him fare."

One or two people on the bus laughed and Grandman continued looking round him. Hill Station, which the Europeans had made for themselves, and where he had made sure he had built one of his own houses; it seemed a bit ramshackle now. The houses were so high up - they looked as if they were going to fall off their perches. And the solitary families still lived there - they had changed names and color, that's all. Afraid, everyone of them. Curfew time and every man jack was in bed tucked under a sheet. But the old man and the passenger tours roamed the streets and Grandman looked for his village.

"Regent," the boy shouted. Grandman got off and the boy peered suspiciously at the money that Grandman had given him. Yes, nothing much had changed. Could he do the same thing again? It depended on Dele really, not them - the bovine creatures for whom he had not the slightest respect - anymore than he had for their masters. If she felt that he could, he would. He would tell them so first. Or perhaps that had changed and now they told you. He thought to himself that one had to sit and wait and listen and then pounce; she would know. Laws, detention, new constitution, a few exiles, then to satisfy the people in the *poda poda* and their families, some seemingly rash but studied generosity on his part. Rice? Flour? He didn't know yet. Perhaps people wanted different things now.

Curfew or no curfew the inmates of Regent Village fenced themselves behind wooden windows and slept till cockcrow. There were thieves; there was *ronshoo* who whistled at nights and carried a gun and money; there was the one-footed devil; there were witches that cried like cats. And people were so wicked. Black thread, kola-nut, sometimes a coffin could be laid across your door in the morning and then where would you be? Unless you had pee to throw over it all. Better to close the windows and not to open doors for rooster or husband. Grandman thought - yes it is not much different. The church is there, high on the hill in darkness, waiting for its Sunday waking. Till then people slept. But he would wake them up - by God and the devil he would. And this time it was not just to make Grandman but a grand people. Would it happen? Was it possible? Soon he would know if he was still dreaming or if he had woken with her into the novelty of a different world. And if prison had made him free.

96

# CHAPTER 8

There are questions, Stephan thought, for which there were no known answers. But what was it that Sarki had said about some answers having no questions? Seems he had gotten things mixed up, at least a little bit. He was with Sarki and they had driven south; seemed like a good thing to do. You got tired of the dusty smell of the North. Dust that lay immobile in the air. It was good to see the green forests here; they always seemed to be slightly damp with a tinge of rain. When they first came to the forests, off the side of the road they could observe a couple, machete over their shoulders, going or coming from their yam gardens. Sarki couldn't resist playing tour guide.

"Here a man's wealth is in yams."

He had only nodded, watching the fool up ahead who was trying to race the wind and would probably end up a casualty. God, he had never seen so many accidents. A man catapulted like a small stone from his car, face downward in a ditch; a woman with blood on her face sitting bolt upright and screaming, "Am I all right? Are you sure?" A twitching piece of flesh on the roadway and a crowd round it; the torso of someone and a lorry-driver spitting and wiping his forehead and crying. Dogs dead at every turn, bellies ripped out, head at a lopsided angle. A new road was needed - a wide one, such as he would build. It would take them from the dry up-country to the wet point of the moving ocean.

In the old days it must have been damn difficult, he reflected, to move from anywhere to anywhere, especially South to North. There wasn't a damn thing resembling a road and then some joker had pieced this one together. Sarki must have been reading his thoughts.

"My people don't want a new road. It will increase the problems we have with the new slave raiders of the South."

"Slave raiders?" Stephan inquired sceptically.

"Yes. They come onto our territories and take our groundnut for nothing

97

and then they come back here and sell it - "

"That's called free enterprise - "

"What about our own culture which is being daily watered down by contact with the Southern Christians? Many of them have forgotten their own real past."

Stephan did not reply; his mind was elsewhere. He was thinking about what Sarki had first said about slave raiders. Yes in some strange, ironical twist of history the old slave catchers were the first pioneers of this road he was thinking of. They knew the meanderings; safe places where the road could branch off to a nearby village; another that was not wedged in between hills so that he could build rest areas, provide accommodation for a hotel.

"They're no hotels now," Stephan exclaimed suddenly, "But later - "

"Yes, weigh stations too for the produce of the North. Don't you see Mr. Hamilton a road is good for the South, not for us. We have suffered in the past when there was no road. Much less now."

Stephan was conscious of the boy's eyes probing his. He looked over and Sarki turned quickly away. Shit! he could say what he wanted. This was an exploratory trip for Stephan to see what was what, what needed detours, which parts should be closed off and returned to the heavy jungle, which parts should be saved and how much new land would now be reclaimed. In a weird way he now had the destiny of those early morning farmers and their wives in his hands. Yes he did. Their farms could be in his control tomorrow, and their children would be looking elsewhere for legacies. The slave's revenge, he thought. The central government had blessed this, and now he was going in for an okay in black and white. Sarki's great-grandfather would have to turn over literally in his grave when he sent the bulldozers in. The scenery continued to run past the window; as monotonous as hell. In the distance out of the dust in the air, he could look down and see the second largest town in the area. Corrugated zinc roofs and white outside walls, meandering streets. A light drizzle began to fall.

"Here we are my brother," he told Sarki.

Sarki had fallen asleep, stretched a little, yawned and said, "Thanks for bringing me a little off your route, my brother."

"Nothing to it. I'll meet you exactly here in two days at the time we agreed."

He let Sarki out near the market place and then stayed for a minute in the shade trying to make sense of what he saw. It was a market day and maybe as many as four or five of the surrounding villages had come together. There was everything in abundance - meat, rice, yams, cassava, grain, salt, chickens protesting from their enclosures, and over it all the noise of men and women. A young boy passed him, turned back and led an old lady up to him. She was blind and the boy held an open calabash. The woman was one of the wandering minstrels and she chanted to the rattle of a hollow gourd with strings attached. It was the same song he had heard that night with Sarki and Cecily Dawn:

> *Every neighbor is my brother, is my sister*
> *Hear oh hear!*

Terribly repetitious people; the songs seemed to be the same in every goddamn place or else they must have their own top ten, and ran through the first one every time they saw a stranger. He tossed a coin in the calabash and the vacant eyes of the old woman neither thanked him nor cursed him. They were just there - vacant eyes until a fluttering of eyelids told him that the boy was leading her on. For just a moment heads were turned towards Stephan as the boy held the old woman's hands, his beads long and hanging down in front of him. Then he was gone. Stephan daubed at his face with a handkerchief. Those were the beads that Dele wore, the same damn beads that she would never take off. She said it had something to do with her religion, whatever the hell that was, and yet here those beads were in Africa, almost in the middle of the damn continent. When he moved off, coasted the car for a while and finally hit the road again, the woman's vacant eyes and the boy's beads, like dozens of eyes shining in the sun, stayed with him.

When he came back, with the signatures, after two days of bureaucratic prevarication, Sarki was waiting for him under a mango tree, eating a mango. A woman was selling mangoes underneath.

"That's what I call hope," Stephan greeted Sarki cheerfully. "A woman on the public highway selling free mangoes - "

"I bought mine," Sarki cut him off. He looked unhappy but it was several miles before he began speaking.

"House to house," he said as if to himself. "The same answer. But I know they're wrong."

"What the hell are you talking about?"

Sarki stared with the vacant eyes of the old woman into the distance. When Stephan glanced down, as if by some quick impulsive apprehension, for the first time he noticed the beads round Sarki's neck. Strange, he thought. I had never looked, never asked and never found out.

"Who's wrong?" again from Stephan.

They still had some miles to go before sundown, and they would stop at a government-owned rest house, and spend the night, and then leave early the next day and try to put as much distance behind them as possible. The dry up-country was still some distance away.

"My great-grandfather was Keeper of the Stables," Sarki said. "He came down to these parts with Queen Shade. He was the one that raped her." He went on in this incomprehensible manner for a long time but Stephan was negotiating his way through some sheep, on the wrong side of the road. As usual there was the carrion of those sacrificed to the road.

"Ogun," Sarki had muttered once, bitterly. "The god of the road, iron and steel. He does this to all people." His hand pointed to the carnage on the road.

"Didn't you say he was a Yoruba god?"

"Yes," from Sarki.

"Well then how do you know about him? How is he part of the religion of a well brought up Muslim boy?"

Sarki slumped in the seat of the car.

"Mr. Hamilton you don't understand anything I have been saying to you." For some reason he remembered the vacant sockets of the blind woman and Sarki's beads that caught the sinking light.

"When my great-grandfather left in the company of Queen Shade, she taught him as she had done her husband, the Emir Mohammed, some of the wisdom of her own Yoruba people. We have been part of all this ever since." History again. Fiction.

"What I learnt in the village was that Queen Shade and her son had died in the forests. No one ever saw them come back. I talked to my fellow priests, especially the fathers of secrets. They say that they never returned."

"So," Stephan compromised amiably as they were getting their stuff from the car and taking it to the rest-house. "They must have died."

"Our priests say differently. The Keeper of the Stables told our ancestors a different story when he came back. He admitted his wrongdoing but before he took his life, he told us that he had hidden when he heard sounds of people coming. That they had the young prince with them and they took the queen - Queen Shade. They were people from her region of the South and they took her with them."

As they were lighting the lamps in the large room, Sarki sat down heavily on the bed, "Unless," he said, "they were slave catchers."

100

"Let's go eat," Stephan said. "There's nothing here."

Sarki knew that this was not true, that they had retraced the path of Queen Shade, that the Keeper of the Stables had raped her near the very stream he saw the previous day, that people had come and taken her away and that these were her own people but those who were being well paid in mirrors and beads (he touched his own beads) to betray their own. Now he fully realized that he must have been right in his own thinking all the time and that both the fathers of secrets and the priests of his religion must have been right. There was only one way to know for certain.

Over dinner Stephan saw Sarki look up suddenly and smile. His eyes were shining in the half dark. "Tonight," Sarki said, "we will sleep together."

The uncomfortable feeling he had had when he first met the boy was there again. He remembered the evening (how long ago it seemed) and the boy's toes and his lean body as he sat outlined against the sky. Stephan buried his face in his food and continued eating thoughtfully.

*     *     *

There was nothing there, the boy thought. Nothing but the sky in the distance like an overturned gourd and the sea working itself into foam. He was frightened but he did not show it for he knew that near him the ancestors walked, and that these men with strange voices and strange words belonged to some land beyond the stretch of that wide blue river. And he would come back. "Boy," a white *oyinbo* once said over him. He did not understand. "Boy" again and the *oyinbo* kicked him and spat his tobacco out sideways from his mouth. That was his name, he thought, and he tried to say it as the *oyinbo* did, at first quietly to himself and then louder. The man at first looked startled and then he smiled, dug his boots in the sand and walked away laughing.

On the shaking house they had strapped pieces of white cloth and the wind hummed round it. He became more aware of his surroundings and he saw others like him, quietly sitting in the sand and looking out. No one said much, for nobody could as yet use new words. It was like the babyhood of the whole world before Obatala had made the first men and Ogun had showed them iron, and Shango, fire. Perhaps it was some odd quirk of misfortune and just a dream that Eshu had played on him - Eshu, the Trickster god who turned men into playthings for his own laughter. He thought he had heard his name but he did not look back. He was so ashamed. Prince Yacub, the son of Emir Mohammed and grandson of the great Emir Sarif and his queen, this very prince must now forsake every attribute of his heritage and go with the already moving house to some other village on the other side of the big blue river.

At night he looked up but there were no stars. Only the dark floor of the roof and the smell of sweat. Now and then he heard the heavy thump of those *oyinbo* men with boots upstairs and the clank of the nearby chains that seemed to do a musical chorus around him. One night an old man cried in his sleep and urinated and by morning had died. The others did not seem to notice him, too preoccupied with their own need for a living. This is how the new village will be, Prince Yacub thought; it will be a village of individuals, no longer a group, of every person who had to fend for himself, secure in his own illusion of liberty, as he sat tied to the next man.

For if now Eshu chose to undo all this - what could he reveal? Could he undo Prince Yacub's own shame and that of his mother's? Could Eshu in his wily manner bring back the serenity of life within the thatches of the village, of the lazy drum sound in the early night, of the kora and the belafong, the chanting sounds of the warriors, fresh from the hunt, of fishermen at dawn, casting their nets into the mysterious depths of little rivers? Could Eshu bring back the early mornings on the river banks wrestling with his age-mates, or the snug evenings lit by firelight under the eyes of the stars when the children sat round and heard the stories of the wisdom and daring of their own ancestors?

And Prince Yacub remembered that the dead are never truly dead. That they are here in the shuffle of a man's foot on the rotting floor of this hole, in the smell of excreta and sweat and urine that flowed past him like a river, in the sweat that poured out of his forehead. And in the palm of his hands as he touched his skin, he noticed for the first time that the stubble had become hair. He was almost a man. Perhaps this was his own initiation and he would go back to the village, triumphant, after this setting out. Then he would be circumcised and could marry and have children. And then, as now, and later he would be someone's child, fresh in the warmth of her arms and then someone's father who too would see his own children grow. No one, his people said, who had outlived his child, can truly be said to have borne a child. As he had outlived his own father, so he would be someone else's grandfather.

Mornings came suddenly, surprisingly. The sky abruptly shot open and the *oyinbo* men with heavy boots came downstairs and shouted. And the procession of people who could not speak moved, as if at a wake, and followed them upstairs, and walked round and round the tall pole with the white flags in some new ritual. Then eagerly he clutched the hard ball of meat which fell into his lap and brought it to his mouth. Just as suddenly he spat it out. It was the meat of the swine, coated with salt. But nearly most of the people he saw chewed on the meat. The *oyinbo* who had given him his name came back and held him roughly by his shoulders. Then he broke up the meat and shoved it into his mouth and blocked his nose. In a sudden fright he swallowed and just as suddenly the food left and came back up when the man had gone his way and made the ground dark again. Like a sick man the boy looked at his brown vomit until he fell asleep sitting up.

The third time when they took him up he thought he saw her.

"Mother," he called in his language. One of the sailors near him looked startled. Perhaps Queen Shade heard his voice but did not turn her head. She must have heard him. But she was being taken down along with some others. And if she was crying, he could not see, for her back was towards him.

Back down in the hole a man about three bodies away stretched out and touched him,

"I know you, son, and speak your language," he said quietly.

He silenced the boy for he had recognized the man.

"This is a slave ship and they are taking us to the village of White men."

"Of the *oyinbo*?"

"Yes those who walk up there," he pointed to the plank. "They are Portuguese. They are taking us with them to their country."

"Countryman," he pleaded. "Is this then no trick of Eshu?"

The man shook his head silently. Then he whispered, "There is a man with us from another village. His name is Cinque. He has a plan so that we can all go back to our village - "

He stopped suddenly and crawled back quickly into his corner. Those feet again from up above and the opening of the hatch, and boots walking and eyes looking. These *oyinbo* could make light and dark. Then more boots and he felt the clean taste of salt water as the sailors poured buckets over them. One stood near him and pointed to the vomit shouting. "Nigger." That must have been the man's name. He was Boy and the man was Nigger. "Nigger," he called back respectfully. He wanted to talk, to show that he too wished for the companionship the other craved, "Boy" and he pointed to himself.

The man shouted at him and then they all went away again.

"How is it Alhaji," he asked the only man to whom he could speak "that they call themselves Niggers?"

The man laughed, "No," he explained "That's you."

"Me?" incredulously. "I am Yacub, a prince, son of - "

Alhaji waved him to silence. "You are now boy like me, and nigger like us all."

"How can this be? How can they change our names?"

"Son, try to rest. We have a plan. We will escape."

"Alhaji," he confessed. "I am frightened."

"This," Alhaji said, "is your initiation, but you go back to no village; no shell will sound for your arrival. I have been to Mecca and Alhaji though I was, prince though you had been, we are now all niggers and boys."

"I think I saw my mother," Prince Yacub said.

"I heard. You will probably not see her again. This ship is going not to Mecca but to the other side of the ocean. There is neither kith nor kin. But I want you always to remember your *oriki*, 'every neighbor is my brother, is my sister.' "

"How can I act Alhaji when I do not know their tongue?"

"You'll see." He pointed. In the distant dark he made out the form of a man of medium build. He was standing and speaking without words, pointing to his chained feet and his wrists and gesticulating.

"That's Cinque. We must follow him now. This very night when the sailors are sleeping, we will all move together - "

"How can we? We who are in chains - "

Alhaji laughed. "Together we can. No man can free himself alone but the chains will bind us together."

He had not thought of it like that before. The chains were for him not a binding force but a fence that kept any two apart.

"And I will see my mother?"

"Who knows? If it is Allah's will . . . "

Alhaji's voice trailed off in the distance. Prince Yacub remembered Alhaji, a man of means in the community. He had been called Alhaji after he had made the *hadj* to Mecca and returned. He had always worn white, immaculate white, always worn in great contrast to the cloth that now barely hid his genitals.

He waited in the dark. Like initiation this would be a test of courage but, as Alhaji had said, there was no going back. This he had to resolve within himself once and for always. The going forward could be to a new life on another shore. A little like living itself; the setting out that was a birth, the journey and initiation of woman and man and the arrival, the victorious coming of those who had not surrendered. That night as he waited he thought of the girls he had hardly noticed before in the village. They came to him and lay over him and let their small breasts lie on his chest as their hands felt his stubble. And suddenly like a rush of rain from below his chest he felt it, his first coming. When he awoke, he knew he was no longer boy. Ahead lay the true test for manhood.

The signal had been passed round. Not tonight but tomorrow. Cinque was not standing now; he could make him out very dimly getting ready to sleep. Prince Yacub passed on the message, gesticulating with his hands. The person on his right was a boy, younger than he was, and he noticed him for the first time. The person who had passed on the message was a sleepy old man with a pointed beard. He did not know these people.

"We are all one people now. We all live in the same village now," Alhaji told him. "This," and he pointed to the color of his hand, "is what makes us one, so Cinque says, and I believe him. We are no longer old nor young. No longer Alhaji, prince or peasant. We are all - "

"Nigger," he ended Alhaji's words. The old man on his left nodded and silently said as if to himself, "Nigger." He had a deep voice, like a drum.

"Is it a new family then?" Prince Yacub asked.

"Yes. We have met in the dark corners of this moving ocean and we are one now. And if anyone seeks to be not one of us, then we must kill him."

He thought about this and then asked, "But Alhaji do we then destroy our own family?"

"Yes my son, we must for the good of all. Tomorrow when we go up for air we will attack the sailors."

Those were the last words he heard Alhaji speak, for the next day when Cinque and Alhaji tried to rush the sailors, they were beaten back. There were shouts of alarm and terror and Cinque freed himself and opened up the hatches where the others were. But no one came up. It was as if they were expecting first to hear those boots, the shouts of the *oyinbo*, before they could move. Still Cinque, the only free man in that prison called a ship, fought. With two bare hands he brought one sailor down and took away his cudgel. The other sailors panicked but they rushed him together. Prince Yacub found himself drawn into the center of it as the two men fought to beat off the sailors. But to no avail. Their weapons were stronger for they pointed their own staff and fire came out and people fell. But not Alhaji, nor Cinque who had already killed two men and who was now making for the sailor with the musket.

Someone must have panicked and he felt himself being drawn back down into that hole again. As he looked back he saw Alhaji fall, alone, in the middle of the deck and he twitched twice and red blood came out of his side. Prince Yacub screamed but no one seemed to notice.

Cinque fought on. Between the feet of the sailors, dodging their blows, taking those he could not avoid. They were still tugging at him and Prince

Yacub felt a taste of pain as he was pushed against the old man. He turned to apologize but saw the old man slump forward moving with the confused bodies that tugged him, dead as Alhaji was dead.

Before they dragged him down, Prince Yacub saw Cinque climb on to the deck and collar one sailor. Another he bludgeoned to death and, before the fire of the musket could get him he leapt as high as a vulture into the sky and down to the infernal bowels of the churning sea. Below the sailors whipped them, then rubbed salt in their wounds and shouted. But Prince Yacub was proud; he had seen one man who dared defy a crew of other men and who, when he realized that he could not win, had thrown himself pell-mell off the moving house and had swum back home. In the dark below the dead man was still secured to him and Prince Yacub felt his cold hands and knew that, like Cinque and Alhaji, he too had gone to join his own ancestors. Only when he remembered his mother did he cry.

*　　*　　*

Usually Stephan was at the site by about seven. The blasting would take place about ten but there were a million chores to do before. He was glad that the new D8 had arrived, one of the larger earth movers; he would send that in after the blasting to clear the road ahead. On site, he went through the daily roll call of his stable crew, some two hundred or so masons, mechanics, plumbers and welders. One of his managers suggested that they have about fifty day laborers that day to expedite the work of clearing the bush, the blasting and the surfacing of the rubble. Work had fallen behind schedule, with what he considered to be a wasted visit to the south, for he had really learned nothing except that people built roads rather badly and that the only thing the central government seemed interested in was the end-product.

Definitely behind schedule. He got up in his small, cramped, dusty office, turned the lever of the overhead fan a little faster and called out. A young woman appeared, pencil and pad on the ready.

"You always seem so efficient," he laughed. "Let's look at the flow chart together. Just help me go over it."

They went to the cream wall, a little stained with use and downright greasy in parts.

"Definitely a little behind," he muttered. "Write down that we'll have to work at maximum for at least a week. And fill in the details for me."

"The foremen and sub-foremen are waiting outside Sir," she reminded him gently, after a messenger had come in and said something to her.

"God!" he said a little irritatedly. "The weeks pass so quickly. Do you know what a road is?" he asked the woman who had been writing and then continued as if to himself, "It's a monument, a people's history in tarmac. Every person who travels there is paying homage to what that architect did or did not do. Every man, woman and child, whether they know it or not, were honoring him for sparing their lives, for building in such a way that they did not become sacrifices to Ogun, catastrophes under clay." His thoughts had drifted off. The secretary stood patiently by, with a half-smile lurking on her face. Looked downright silly, he thought.

Damn it! He felt uncomfortable as he went outside to the noise of the foremen. The flow chart had called for a specific mileage of roadway each day and he had not really kept up with it. He would build this road despite himself, the slovenliness of some of his workers, the callousness of his home base; you name the problem and he had it. Boots firmly on, he talked for a full half hour to his men, about the need for safety. Today there was need to have blasting crews again. He did not want any given crew of men within a two hundred yard range when blasting was in progress. He talked a little about his journey south but no one seemed interested. There was nothing there, he said. Nothing he could really learn.

"If we're blasting here," he reminded the foremen of the blasting crews again, "remember my illustration on the road and the flags we have put down." He wiped beads of perspiration from his forehead, reached out for a glass of water, did not like the taste but bravely swallowed. "We've put those markers down so that," and he sketched the rest on the board, the hill ahead and the decline veering off to the west. "We blast here," he pointed to the hill, "but only in quantities large enough to fill this. Then," he glanced round as some of the faces of the clearing-up crew tightened, "you go in after a decent interval. With the earth movers you go this way," he pointed, "and dump this way." He looked round; anxious faces, stern faces, apprehensive faces, proud faces, faces of warriors, clowns, local doctors, priests. Perhaps they too cared or would they sit through so patiently as if they had not heard this before, when he had gone it over time and time again? Suddenly he began to be a little envious of them; they would be around when the road was completed; they would be able to say to their children that they had helped build it. By then his role in it would be largely forgotten, relegated to the background with a phrase such as "a Black expatriate" or "a man from America," if he were mentioned at all. Then he felt ashamed that he sought to take away from them their moments of memory, their illusions that they would bequeath their children. After all he had always said that this was just a job, like any other job for which he would be paid. The rest was null. History is a trap in which people fell because they tried to look to the future as if it were the past and because they based all their actions for the future on compromise. He had little use for history. Or for bequeathals.

"Today I'll be round on an inspection meeting."

The session broke up; one or two people stayed back to talk with him, to iron out some last minute details. Then he went into the hot office and tried to get right under the fan, staring at the flow chart, also a belief in the possibilities of the future, but a belief again that had not materialized. Then again he thought how the purpose of his meeting strangely, that very morning, had been a confirmation that there was this predestined future and that the present could alter so dramatically that it affected the future in no uncertain terms. For some reason Sarki jumped into his mind, irrelevantly, when he was driving the landrover. There were some hazards, he thought, further up. These would have to be cleared before blasting began tomorrow - piles of junk, some cattleman's temporary shelter, a disused oil drum. One of the men ran up to him and he stopped. Equipment had been stolen during the previous night.

"Make a note," Stephan said. "Find out if it was secure and change the lock on the trailer."

The order would be passed down. It was as if he were in his own village, elected as a king or *oba*, as Sarki would have said. Perhaps the people at site headquarters would have an Emir and Frost was their emissary. That's all, just another messenger, like the guy in his office. Back in the office he looked through his correspondence, dictated his letters and was about to split for lunch when he remembered something.

"Order ten tons of five-eighths steel," he said. "And could you try to get the cement out of bond?"

She nodded; it was getting hotter. Stephan thought that he ought to have a last look at the beginnings of the road before the blasting started. Once the cement was in, the tar in the solidified barrels, already half melting in the sun, would have to be poured. The sewage, water and electricity had already been laid down, with the sand coating the pipes. No shortage of sand here. On top was gravel, more sand over that and he had packed dirt, heavy rocks, more sand and then mall over that. Each layer had been gone over by rollers of the paving crew. In a few days they would be near the cemetery and he would repeat the process; survey teams, clearing crews, then blasting cutting and filling and then

108

the whole thing sprayed over with liquid tar. Sarki's great-grandfather would be tightly packed for all time between six inch layers of sand and gravel, and the rain and the rollers would preserve him for history, he thought whimsically.

"Old man can you help yourself? Where will your history be when I send the electrical cables pass your ass and run sewage pipes near your nose? Then cover it all over with black tar and trim the edges nicely with gravel near the shoulder of the road and plant grass further in? You could not even erode, old man, could not even wind with the road and disappear with the rains."

He saw Sarki ahead; a light rain was falling as he drove and pulled over. He stopped. Sarki looked up terrified.

"No," he waved Stephan on. "You must not be friends with me."

"What?" Crazy nigger!

Sarki walked on. Stephan got out of the car and held on to him near the side of the road. The priest did not struggle. "I know what you're doing and you're right. My ancestor was evil to you; this is why you wish to desecrate his grave."

"But you said," Stephan gently reminded him with a half-laugh, "that your people believe that the ancestors are always alive."

"The flesh was his house once. Destroy it if you will. What he did was not good. He raped your great-grandmother."

The priest disappeared into the light drizzle.

*　　*　　*

Dele found herself in a large room. In the corner there had been erected elaborate altars which were set up to honor the gods. On the shelves to the left of her and just behind the santéro in front of whom she was seated, the colors, the beads, the symbols and the large tureens in which the qualities of the various gods were contained. The santéro said quietly as if to a child, "It is better sometimes not to know my child," and then he fingered the cowrie shells which were in his hands. He muttered this very quietly and she sat there still, almost as still as the child that she remembered who had sat and had observed the young bald priest as he had led the procession of worshippers. She recalled the possessed woman who had screeched with a voice her own and yet not her own. Overhead the fan turned quietly on the ceiling and she saw the shadows of light playing on the white tablecloth.

"What do you see?" petulantly from her.

"It is difficult to tell," he replied soberly.

First he cast the shells. When she saw them fall, some open with their jagged teeth pointing upward, some closed with the round smooth line of their backs on the tablecloth, he studied them but said nothing for a long time. He looked at her, muttered almost to himself, but she could hear nothing for he was saying what he had said in a tongue which she had not known. Again he cast the shells and this time he chanted quietly, quietly, to himself again. Her first reaction was almost terror. Although she did not understand fully what number had come up, she thought she had read a kind of vacant horror in his face; but then his face was almost always expressionless and she could not be sure. To the right on the top shelf of the altar the creator god, Obatala, smiled down at her, or so she thought. Perhaps it would not be so bad after all, perhaps the secret that the diviner held so delicately, like a finely tuned instrument in his knuckles, perhaps this secret would not be so terrible. She, who had come to see her own past, and to know something of her own future, must now face squarely the present; and this present was as obscure as it was terrifying for her. Outside she thought she heard the small tiny drum sounds and the quiet singing of people at a *bembe*. It was nothing really, just a feast, just a celebration, not the religious fervor nor the ecstasy which would follow later. After the drinks and the music and the sound of the drums, after the singing and the laughter and the dancing, as women wriggled themselves smoothly like snakes and men stamped on the iron ground with heavy feet, there would be the rituals, there would be the confrontations with the gods. But for now -

"It is better not to know," he said again.

Knowing, she thought, can only be a little worse than not knowing. The difference between knowing and not knowing was perhaps only the pain that one felt from truth. Yes it was sometimes better not to know, not to have to feel the ague, not to have to experience the low moment of deep anxiety, not to have to question the rustle of the curtains behind her, nor to have to look askance at the gods who were before her. To know was to experience in one moment of time a truth that could be bitter, but one which nevertheless had been always there, always, like Stephan's hands caressing her thighs, or Stephan and his eyes boring into her very soul or even Pietro with his kind acts. She had come of her own free will because for her this was no idle moment of perfection but a true glory that she felt deep within her, because the rustling of the curtain and the silent drum beat outside came together in one moment of time as the santéro spoke.

"Your mother and your grandmother they are almost the same," he said quietly, staring at the cowrie shells which were still on the table. "Your grandmother and your mother were almost the same."

What could she make out of all this? What kind of answer should her tongue form to the riddle that the santéro stated? If she were allowed to speak she might have asked any one of a hundred things. How? Why? My mother, she might have said, was a woman who was young; yes, I remember her, she was a beautiful woman, a woman who had loved me through my entire childhood and died before she had known me grown. She might have said: I never knew my grandmother and this riddle that you tell me, santéro, is no riddle; this makes little sense to me. You are the very santero, now grown older, now wiser, now given the power to interpret the secrets of Ifa. His sounds broke into her thoughts:

"I see a queen." For a moment he stopped and seemed to be looking at her with his eyes and yet to be reading some secret that lay very deep within the closed confines of the cowrie shells. The cowrie shells were shaped, she thought, like a womb, like her womb, but they too had to surrender their secrets, as her womb would, when the time was ready. Now, as delicate as any surgeon's fingers, the santéro moved his hands slowly over the cowrie shells, and continued, "I see an ancestor, raped, yes I see her raped by someone who was not her equal. There is a stream nearby; there are people who come up and there is a running footstep of a child crying in terror."

So her ancestor had been a slave. That much she had already known before she had come. Queen? No, she could hardly believe this herself. But her initiation into santeria and the long year she had spent in white, her head shaven, obeying the whims of this very santéro before her, had taught her that he must be right. She remembered her mother; her mother had jet black hair and she used to tell her of someone that she had known when she was younger. Strange, she thought, there had never been any mention of a father. She had grown up almost thinking that she had tumbled into the world out of nowhere much like the cowrie shells had fallen out of the santéro's hands onto the white tablecloth. But then her religion had told her that beneath the fall of those shells, beneath her unawareness of what had taken place in her life before she had opened her eyes, there was this secret hidden in the very bowels of her mother and the intestines of these shells.

"Your grandmother and your mother were both friendly with the same man," he continued in a blind voice. "Your grandmother was the daughter of this woman I see fighting for her life in the forest. Your grandmother was the product of this rape. That much I see."

Suddenly she felt as if she had heard enough. She had the impetuous desire to run away, to get back to the security of what she thought she knew. Suddenly she seemed to be afraid of those dark secrets. The unexplored interior of those cowrie shells. The thing she remembered was that truth was a bitter weapon; that she had come attempting to find out whom she was, something which had been promised her a long time ago. That was the time when they had brought her out after her year in white, with head shaven, and when her own god had said that she too would soon know the truth about herself. She knew that all along she had dreaded this encounter, that all along she had prefered to pretend that there was no alternative to her life, and that what she had chosen for herself was all round her. The very material world of San Francisco and Stephan and Pietro and her job - that this was reality. Each time she clutched those beads around her, each time she felt them round her neck, she remembered what Shango had promised her at her own initiation. Shango, the god of Thunder and Lightning, was to her the god who sounded out truth the loudest and who ferreted out the dark corners of mystery with a searching light. This was why on a rainy day when the lightning struck from overhead and thunder roared, she had come to this holy man, to find her own peace.

"Your ancestor," his voice droned on, "was a queen. In a way what I see for you," suddenly his eyes seem to narrow themselves down so that they almost became one, "what I see here in these shells is that your grandmother's doing, and your mother's doing, are also yours.

Again there was this longing to ask a million questions. How could she, she wondered, escape from the entrapment of her own history? Was it indeed better not to know as the santéro had said? Was it better, perhaps, like Stephan, to say that there was not another knowing, that history was just a trap? For a moment again there was that impulse to run away, to dart away from the piercing eyes of the god behind the santéro and to move quickly away from the rustle of the curtain and to think that this was what she wanted, that the streets hurtling themselves down, and the peal of bells and the wave-washed shore were all that mattered, since it was a moment of time she could perceive, understand and dispel. But then the nagging feeling that the alternative, her history, could not be discovered in this cavalier manner, that if she did run she had to come back seeking to know a truth that did not lie out there, that honesty lay before her now, as the santéro intoned the verses of the Yoruba lines which accompanied the numbers which had come out.

Why would she have to be much as her mother and grandmother had been? Was it so difficult after all to escape the clawing hands of past? Was it an impossibility to elude the grim fingers of history that pointed inexorably in one direction and one only? She had been thought to believe in destiny; that Obatala had parceled up her life for her in some strange manner that suited some quirk of his mood at a given moment. Like when he had got drunk and created albinos and hunchbacks. And when he had laughed because he had done this. She dared not ask a question, for she knew that her voice, any voice, would break the spider's web, the thread-like link, which the diviner had so deftly woven between them and the other world. For now he was not just the man she knew who sat before her; he was the spokesman for the oracle and through him she would hear what had been, what was and what would be for her.

"Be careful of those who walk with you," he said, a little louder this time. " 'Every neighbor is my brother, is my sister.' This is what the oracle said."

Suddenly he shot up, retrieved the cowrie shells and turned his back on her and before her hands could move from off the table, before she herself had time to form a single question which she knew she must not, he had gone; behind the silk curtain, away from the sound of the quiet drums and the singing and the fan that spun webs over her and the blank white tablecloth which fixed her eyes with an inscrutable interrogative. Then from nowhere came a voice - his voice? She did not know. She was hurt and confused and worried and muddled all at the same time, and she remembered wondering at that time how real all this was and if indeed, as Stephan had said, history was a trap. The voice came almost like an echo, "I see bread and darkness, palm oil and wind, water and rain." She did not understand and in her mind there was the desire for further fulfillment. The questions kept coming back. Now perhaps she could ask and she did.

"Tell me Father of Secrets, why must I retread that same path?"

"Because you are your ancestor's child. As your grandmother was born out of an unnatural union between a commoner and the queen, as your grandmother and your mother both knew the same planter, the same Spaniard whose wealth was in tobacco, so you too will repeat the mistakes of those generations."

The room was darker now, she noticed, and for the first time she felt a strange relaxation in her body. It was almost as if she had been told not only the truth about herself but had been given some strange medicine that enabled her to live with its poison. The past, she realized, was not in any one moment of time but was for all time. The present was not now but then and also tomorrow and the day after.

To try to seek the answers to the questions that she had asked, she had to understand not only herself and the child that lay quietly in her, but she had to know that this very self was no mere caprice. This self had been predestined in a time that was now and then and forever. If she sought to seek that time (and she did) then the going back was a going forward. Like the slaves' journey as she now realized. Her ancestor did not know which way that ship was heading; she had no idea whether in fact the ship was moving at all. Perhaps she had thought that it was a still village and the people dwelt there forever. So her going forward was nothing that she herself knew, nothing that she could instinctively comprehend. When she had left her native shore in Africa and gone to Cuba, the realization of what she was doing was only understood by Dele at a later time. Those names - Africa, Cuba - were meaningless in the context of her ancestor's journey. She had known, as the santéro had said, that she had been raped; as Dele herself had been despoiled. She had known that there was some kind of going forward to another life, perhaps, perhaps not. But if she wondered in those still twilight hours, or if as she lay under the deck of the ship in the constant dark, if she wondered at all, then she could only know what Dele herself had not known until now. And that was this: She realized fully now that she was trapped in a dark hole, with strange people, waiting . . . much as Dele's child was waiting . . . much as Dele herself had waited on that eventful evening years ago when she had, *iyawo* as she then was, become the new bride of Shango. The secret of the cowrie shells was surely this: that in the round enclosures of their being, in the secret corners and hidden passageways, there was an absolute moment when all time stood still. When man had not yet been created and yet was in full bloom; when Dele's child had not yet been born and yet was an old woman or man with bent back hobbling over a weak stick. When her ancestor, her grandmother and her mother, and herself were still part of the secret ways of the world and nothing had any meaning yet, no meaning that is that any of them could yet understand.

By now the room was very dark; the drumming had stopped and in the distance there was still the sound of Shango making his message clear from the skies. When the lightning flashed and the thunder sounded again almost under the table and round her feet, she felt for the first time her child turn within her womb. And Dele knew then that her life, her child's life, the lives of those who had been before her and indeed everyone else's, were intertwined in a curious umbilical cord which stretched, like a cosmic cobweb, to the ends of the world itself. For no reason at all she remembered Stephan and she realized, as the lightning lit the eyes of the gods sitting on the altar in front of her, in one short moment of time, she knew that Stephan could never be her husband. For their

114

destinies had been too close, and when he finally came to some meeting place, any meeting place, where he would know what and whom he was, he would realize that the curved secrets of the cowrie and the hidden life in the womb were one. And that this child, his own and yet not his own, would never call him father. For they had come out of the same womb, from the primordial crime of the strange man who had raped her ancestor, of the incest between her grandmother and the planter, her mother and that same man, all had been passed down. She too had been a victim of this incest for had she not slept with her own brother?

As she ran out of the room towards the drizzle of the street and the lights which seem to gleam like tears, she heard the mocking voice:

> Every neighbor is my brother, is my sister
> Hear oh hear.

# CHAPTER 9

In Iota night smells; it smells with the smell of pain that pricks and makes a man greedy for living and love, for the essence of hope and all desire that is forever beyond reach. Night tastes of red flames that once were fresh, of forgotten ecstasies that one human tongue cannot savour nor two mortal lips relish. Appetite for the eternal is whetted, for ideals and the unrealized that lie' half forgotten in the backyard of childhood, for feelings, which exalt and transpose, immortalize and deify to step-ladder heights of daring. Poetry is in a woman's shoesole, in the last half-sentence a small child says to a companion, in three brown sheep-droppings that dot the tar-road. In the fall and press of night and in its very womb themes are born and music is heard by those whose feelings twenty-six letters can never express. It is the time of Heaven, when darkness reaches down from up, and God's drums become some men's - the dream of creating. But others have always known, for they belong to sleeplessness, fear and hunger; a cripple is the nightmare of God.

The cripple paddled along B line on her hands and knees. She had pieces of car tire strapped to her knees and wore open sandals under her palms, kept in place by straps around her fingers. Her thin misshapen legs curved up behind her loose feet bobbing up and down as she crept along the street. When she got near a streetlamp she stopped and hoisted her back up against it. Her thin beautiful face received the light like a halo and her ear-rings shone. She took out a bowl and placed it in the sandy road; feet carefully avoided her. She said in a thin squeaky voice: "Dash, dash."

No one observed her. The wheels of a cyclist churned up dust in her face and the feet of running children stirred up the ground. Other feet passed too; no different; one man's footsteps are much like another's at night when dreams wake. "Money for food," the cripple called.

The feet of the town passed her by; bare feet, straight feet, thin legs, paralytic

117

legs. Feet are feet and footsteps only measure the gait of the world. Under the street-lamp, out of the liquid darkness running feet irritated the ground. The cripple heard someone panting near her, then a food packet, a brown paper packet tied with string was thrown into her bowl. She looked up quickly but the feet were gone. Others came, perhaps another one running. She did not know. She covered her bowl and crept away into the darkness.

*  *  *

It was late evening when Dr. Pietro had walked into the compound from the street; doors protected it from the cyclists and donkeys, beggars and handcarts, pedestrians and goats that passed at all hours of the day and night. To get into the compound one either walked through the street doors, each of which was a private dwelling, or one used the side entrance near the rubbish dump. The man came quickly through the side-entrance, almost nervously, like someone hiding. A cripple watched him from the ground. The compound was almost deserted; three children played at the far corner in the dust and a turkey-cock pecked irregularly at the mud.

In the compound were six more rooms and opposite each one white charred outhouses which were the kitchens. The man stopped as he walked across the compound and looked back over his shoulder: he saw a cyclist pass the sidedoor. The cripple crept past on her hands and knees; early evening discolored the perimeter of the entrance and a radio played somewhere close at hand. The man went up to the last door and rapped softly. The children stopped playing in the dust and looked at him, silently. He turned his face away as a mosquito quietly hummed past his ears. He knocked again, a little louder this time, with a trace of irritation. Drops of blood began to appear at his feet.

He tried the door and noticed that it opened. He pushed back the curtain and went into a dark room. When his eyes got accustomed to the darkness, they could pick out a table with two chairs and some dirty plates on them, two chairs and a small radio set. At one end another curtain separated it from another room.

"Sunday," he called softly.

A voice muttered something indistinct in the adjacent room. The man went through the curtain quickly. In the darkness of the other room a young boy of about seventeen was lying on a bare mattress. The upper part of his body was naked.

"Sunday," the man said. "I came as soon as I heard. I just got back."

118

In the darkness the boy opened his eyes; the man bent down and looked closer at him. He took a stethoscope out of his pocket and began to examine the boy. Then he asked, "No light?"

There was a trace of irritation in his voice, perhaps from his own pain. The boy turned over on his back with a groan. His bare back-bone was hard against the mattress; the muscle of his right arm bulged at his side.

The man found a lamp, groped in his pocket for matches and lit it. Then he brought it nearer the bed. The boy turned his face round.

"Dr. Pietro," he muttered almost indistinctly. "You are wounded."

"Don't talk," the other replied. "Lie down."

He brought out a thermometer and took the boy's temperature, turning him over on his back to do this. His delicate left hand rounded itself around the curve of the boy's mouth while his right held the thermometer. His eyes were vacant. He took the thermometer nearer the lamp and examined it. Then he returned to the bed, feeling faint.

"Sunday," he said softly. "You have to go to hospital." Sunday did not reply. Dr. Pietro bent nearer his head. The curve of his lips touched the lobe of Sunday's ear.

"Hospital," he whispered. "Hospital . . . "

The youth on the bed turned away groaning.

"You're very ill - "

"Injection! Give me an injection!" Sunday whispered. His voice seemed to be coming from far away.

"It's not enough," Dr. Pietro began weakly.

"Injection!" Sunday repeated. His voice broke as he said this. He tried to raise his head. The doctor stroked his hair gently. "Turn over," he whispered.

Sunday did not hear. The doctor held his shoulders. His thin small fingers massaged the curvature of flesh and bone. He turned him over gently on his face. The doctor tugged at the trouser top but it was too tight. Nervously his hands slid under Sunday's body and undid two buttons. Then he lowered the trousers exposing the upper half of his bottom. The doctor took an injection needle out of his pocket. His hands gently massaged the top of Sunday's bottom, coaxing the bulge. Then he plunged in the needle with weak hands. Sunday groaned slightly. The doctor pulled up the trousers again and replaced the needle in his pocket. He went out on tip-toe, closing the door after him. He looked hastily into the street before he stepped out and walked quickly away. The cripple on her hands and knees watched him go from the dark dust of the street, drops of blood marking out a trail. She saw him collapse and roll over at the corner.

\*　　\*　　\*

Old men die and boys too. But the old men that the boys become are pall-bearers of unwilling bodies during a life-time of corpses. The longer I remained, the more I realized that the boy Stephan had died. I was being born into Grandman and I had no idea what this meant but I knew that I could do it only without Dele. There were no tears, I remember. Dele said "Bye-bye" just the way I had taught her and then she went on a curious-looking *podo-podo*, one of those contraptions with an engine in front and a kind of extended carton behind in which the passengers huddled.

I can't remember now why it was so necessary that she should leave at that time. I do remember that I had just come out from America and it was the time of my first car and my first senior cook. I would come in and say little. There was not much to tell her that she could understand about files and a nagging boss and office messengers. I tried to tell her about the other Dele, but I ate alone and we slept together.

This is not to say that I did not enjoy her. The nights were beautiful and her body at the time was lithe and the bed made little noises out there in the bush where we lived far from the town. She knew how to twist and turn herself into a hundred ways and how to wake me up with teasing. She used to goad me into beating her; she wanted it, so badly that she would say, "Now you must force me." I used to, with her hands tied behind her and my fist over her face, until I had her struggling under me and really trying to scream because she wanted air. I told her I would cure her of sex; I was young then. I did not know that a woman's hole is the grave you dig at with your groins. She did not die. But Grandman was born from Stephan.

For Chrissake, I was no child and she knew that I had a wife. That was another strange thing - how I had married this wife. One day walking in the park - it was summer I believe - I met this young girl. I spoke to her. At first she would not answer - you know how they are, but finally it must have been the utter loneliness in my voice that made her reply. The first time I beat her I told her that she had only spoken to me because she thought I was a cripple. Anyway she was all ART, in large capitals. I liked it and her jeans and long hair and kissing her in the rain because she had to go home after our first week-end and her parents would not really have approved.

When she was eighteen, she came to live with me. Now I thought, they are a funny race. She gives up that nice house in suburbia with Mummy and Daddy for what? For a poky little room behind what used to be a shop. And the strange thing was she seemed to like it. I liked her for different reasons; she was the purest thing I had ever touched. The first time I had sex with her, she chewed gum throughout the whole proceedings. A slur on my manhood, I thought. Or is this my first true cold woman? It was great - I had met so many hot-blooded ones before. Ianty thought I must be losing my grip when I told him.

At the time I was escaping in every sense of the word. Three, maybe four years ago I had fallen in love with Elma. Tall, long toenails (I made her stop painting them), twice married. We had met in - of all places - a cinema in Harlem. Her husband was a sea-man - he had gone to India and Elma and Dele are always the kind of women I love because they harm me. The others like the shy, clean American girl I married, I only respect.

Elma told me first to move in with her. This I did. Christ, the things you do then in young-time! One day - a bright Sunday - I am knocking back the old bacon and eggs then thud thud thud. A knock on the door. Sweet as honey Elma asks, "Who's that?" When the voice replied that it was your husband, darling, there was only one thing to do. Pack in five minutes while she kept up an inane conversation about being in the bath and head for the window. Thankfully it was on the first floor. Not far to jump and away to the nearest subway and then to Ianty's house panting like hell. She went back to him. I always wondered how she explained the contraceptives.

Of course I was an ass or it was sex that made it sweet. Darling went to the high seas again and I repeated the performance - this time minus suitcase. As a matter of fact I was really and truly in the shit now. At least that is how I talk now. For then it was all flowers. She came to live with me. We went to a house, I remember, owned by this old poppa - a Jamaican. He said we could have the front room, but they wanted to play hymns on Sunday. He would deduct ten dollars for that. We agreed. But my God, can you imagine how awful it is when you are in the middle of a good screw to have a whole pack of Jamaicans stroll through (watch you pitifully naked on the bed with a woman) and begin after a formal "good afternoon" to sing lustily to God in his glory? It wasn't worth the deduction and maybe it was this, maybe it was another thing, maybe it was the girl that Grandfather had loved - anyway Elma cleared out. And that was that - people's lives don't criss-cross like in good novels. I am not ashamed to say that I looked for her (Ianty thought me a fool) but I couldn't find her. Soon afterwards I met this girl in the park and I married her. I mean you've got to marry sometime - everybody does.

After I came back to Iota I forgot about this girl I married. I believe she had had a child for me. It's easy to forget when someone is not there that she had ever really been there. I had to find a house, sign an inventory, argue with various people that I was entitled to a larger fan. Meantime Dele was there - she had no clue about anything. She was good for the nights; day-time you felt she was just wasted. I suppose this girl I married expected that she would follow. Maybe I said it, maybe I didn't. I don't think I am a heartless bastard. There are many worse, I can tell you that. This girl used to write me about "fidelity" and "honor" - strange things and her letters had that peculiar scent of her vagina. She did not put it quite so crudely; she said that she was keeping everything for me. She used to send blotting paper through the post, so I would remember her, she said. I used to wonder for what. I mean for Chrissake, so I married her. What was the fuss about? She always took life too seriously. Even her horrible ugly sketches on the wall she chose to term "art" (no capitals this time).

I kept a letter she wrote me when her father died. It was a strange letter because it said so little. I almost gave up and went back to her. She was definitely alone now and in that country even God is hostile. There is neither aunt, uncle nor small brother with nothing to do of whom you can make a kind of lover. Everybody has got his own life worked out. I wonder what happened to that child, if there was one? I wonder what became of her father, after he died.

I remember when Poppa came to the end of his shift. For all his life he had bicycled to the factory. Early morning even before anyone was up - he would take the sandwiches he had made the night before. Food was expensive during the war. Everything had to be concentrated on winning and he would help all he can. I remember those peculiar little faded pictures he had shown me. He wore Bavarian leather breeches and he laughed with uncles who had died on their farms during the bombings. This was the other side to the White people's palaver which I never knew. And there were some girls in those pictures; girls who must be at least a hundred and twenty now. He had left the farm when he was still twenty. His father was dead. There were twenty or was it ten children? Josef wanted all if he could get it and so Poppa's mother had felt that it would be better for Poppa to go. He went. About his death the girl in jeans had written:

"Poppa died so that the lawns would be tidy. Today is the day after the funeral. We had the church service at eleven in the morning and we buried him at one. He died three days before at half-past four in the afternoon. He felt no pain since last week and for him to hear, you had to scream. We were all there when he died - even Aunt Zenda who had come to visit him. I arranged everything as there was no one else and people did not seem to want to know. He had a second class funeral - you know the cheap one you used to laugh at. Everything was done nicely - lots of flowers, lots of people, lots of crying, etc.

"We wanted to see him in the morgue but he looked so ugly and got so swollen up that we had to close the coffin for the funeral. The smell was something terrible. Did you know he had a hole down his side from the radium treatment? Well that was that. He was buried and the relatives had a meal afterwards, although he had said that he did not want this. They did it in true style plus the photograph, which I am sending you. I went home early to look after the child whom I had left with Mrs. Gluck. She says hello and wonders when you're coming back.

"And that's really all. Now I have to wait until the court meets which is sometime next week to decide how it's all going to be divided up. How are things with you? Are you still the same and do you still have hopes of becoming the Prime Minister or whatever it was you said you would become when you went back? There was something on television the other night about Ianty (is he the same student?) and Iota before Poppa died. I kept hoping they would mention your name."

I thought that was the last letter I would have from her. After that I supposed she would just disappear somewhere in Europe. Perhaps she could marry again. Did she understand, I wonder? Perhaps she only understood that I was selfish. Perhaps she only understood that a White woman could not really be by a man's side if he wanted to successfully lead a people (colored differently). She opted out. There was never any quarrel. Often I used to wonder (bloody hypocrite!) what became of her? And what happened to this child - was it a boy or a girl? I had forgotten. It did not seem important then.

I had always felt that I had been bound for some crucial ceremony where the dead preside over the corpses of the living and we are all involved in a last spasmodic effort of will. It wasn't arranged - it simply seemed inevitable. Perhaps Ianty and I took ourselves too seriously as young men. I know I certainly did, even the day that Dele left.

I could not cry although I wanted to cry and laugh all at the same time. I wanted to show Dele that I cared, but she just simply had to go because love is not death everlasting and these barricades that two people erect against misfortune are temporary ones. After the civil wars of the heart, the streets are cleared of rubble and the dead get up and go back to linger outside the cemetery.

Crying was easy; you simply bawled with your mouth (and you looked

123

ugly like hell) - I used to look at myself in the mirror when engaged in this delicate operation, which took place not infrequently with Elma. But the not-crying is not easy. Your eyes are blurred and you wait to hear the silent shuffle of the footfall on the porch which you know you will never hear. Not much of my home-made philosophy there. That statement was as bare as Grandfather's gums.

He had never cried. This strange man from up the river who steered the ferry-boat. He had always won and like Poppa I am sure he ranged death up next to him and said that he would fight him for all he was worth. Of course one knew the result - odd things like water in the knee, and an open wound that won't heal make doctors shake their heads and silently affirm, "We'll do what we can." Which is of course complete rubbish. They know just what will happen. They are the attendants of death - the damn bastards! Pietro taught me that much.

Death and dying have preoccupied me ever since. There was only one way to live - to become everybody's grandfather. *You see now why Stephan had to become Grandman?* The change was crude and sudden but not lightly undertaken. I tried out the signature on endless bits of paper. It seemed right for a great man. And there must be no mistake about this; Grandman was going to be - all right I will say it - a slightly dishonest croupier. People were numbers and one had to juggle them up and down, backwards and forwards. And then one was safe. It was necessary to erect a whole hocus-pocus of ideology round one - for the educated ones, schools, hospitals, roads, industries; for the others, free food, free clothing, free booze. I said it all and they clapped. Next it was necessary to become a political prisoner. The government was most co-operative.

At first the governor had sent for Ianty and me, but Ianty was afraid to go so I went up the sand drive that curved past hedges where the three-storied house was modestly hidden away. The people started chanting what I had told them. The governor was no fool. Before I had met him it was easy to think that he was, but sitting down to lunch (with the boys chanting nearby) and wifey doing the small services like saying, "You must have a fresh napkin." I thought that one damn day he would be out of this house and I would be in. Those rooms of his - what did he have in them? What did the pictures hung up on the wall mean? And the specially-woven local cloth? Couldn't he buy a good carpet from overseas?

He was speaking to me, he said, not as governor, but as a friend. I should lay off! Play it cool! He did not put it that crudely but in his starchy English.

124

Iota would be independent in four, perhaps five years at most and I had the makings of a leader. Who was this little backstreet English boy with his knighthood to tell me about leadership? I got drunk and I told him to kiss my ass and his wife to kiss somewhere else. After the dinner I saw the inside of the prison for the first time. But the boys were chanting for me in the street that time. I made the national and international press. I believe they even sent a few soldiers to seduce the girls and carry out their duty. In prison I began organizing active defense. That was where I met a defrocked (was he ever frocked?) reverend for the first time. The others called him Rev. Two-for-Three. He became our little opposition help! Thus was the two-party system ushered in.

*     *     *

The Manager of Paradise leant over the bar and philosophized with one of his customers.

"Them shoot the barman," and then he added, "I think."

The customers made no comment. Any word these days could be construed in any way. It was better to sip and be silent. One man, who wore a tie and a suit said, however, a little vehemently:

"It been better when them White man dem been dey na this country - lock up the whole damn lot."

"You think say White man go lock up evėry person," the Manager asked, wiping a dead fly off a dirty counter. "People longtime them no been care. Now na different thing."

The man with the tie grew excited. "Na small people can make trouble. We own history na story about holigans, dem rary-boys."

"Them dey fight na here, this same spot where I stand up," the Manager expostulated. "Them shoot that doctor near this same place."

"Because of women," another man with glasses said. "If them tell you make you no go na street, no go na street. What thing is he looking for? Woman?"

The Manager did not reply. In his heart he knew how wrong all this was and he knew too that anything that he said might be reported and that he himself would have to face the long corridors at nightfall and the empty room, except for chamber-pot and bed, if he spoke. In his heart he knew that this was not true, that things happen and people were caught up in the happening and did not know. And they spoke about them and lived in them, but still what they said did not make sense because in the final decision they did not analyze. It was things, not people that happened. People only endured, fornicated and died.

"We get one dirge in we language," the man with the tie said, "The earth does not ever grow fat. You think them people here them know that? Let them kill."

The Manager thought of the earth and the brown soil that was turned over at funerals and the ceremonial lowering of the dead. When he went to his circumcision ceremony, it was not supposed to be like this. The group was all united and they would meet later in another town. Death was easy: Closed eyes only meant the rejection of this town; it was a signal to the initiated that in another town the dead man was living. "I think say that two men ask Dele for go with dem," the Manager said. He was thinking of something else. That this was only the start. The view from the hill-top no longer be the green view, and a view, and a bay that curved into a c. No longer the pencil point of horizon where the edge of land met the sea and the sky fell in wonder not far out from the reach of your hand. Now the view was of smoke rising - smoke signals, the enemy was coming. Later on gun-smoke from the edge of shore near the chopped sea.

"The man na ordinary mortal man like we," he suggested as he served the man in glasses. A whisky in these times, my brother? You don't know what I have seen. After what had happened in other places, anything could happen here too. Those bastards felt that they were above it all. Talk, talk, talk. When you give power to people like Sir Ianty and Two-for-Three, what the hell did you expect? You lock up a good man like Grandman.

A shoe-shine boy came running into the bar and almost jolted him. He threw himself at the feet of the tubby man with glasses and yelled, "They release Grandman, he done kommot na jail." Then for no reason he began to shine the man's shoes furiously. "Is calf-leather. Nice? Is good. From overseas you buy am, not here. Since they lock up Grandman, thing no good na here."

In the distance and coming slowly towards them they could hear the sounds of street-fighting. The Manager thought to himself that he knew that sound.

"I dey close me bar, pay and leave."

The shoe-shine boy laughed, "You blasted man! You think we no know you dey sell the country. Lock am and we go open am." He stood up and everyone looked at him, "Yes we form a revolutionary council with Grandman as head. Now it work for all man. No more damn shoe-shining, you blasted

126

capitalist."

Like a madman he leapt on to the counter and began to polish the Manager's face furiously. "You bastard," he screamed, "I will make you Brown." Then irrelevantly, "No party no dey again. Long live Grandman!" The Manager was thrown down into a corner near the refuse when the street-fighters came nearer. Perhaps it was as well. So Grandman was the hero of the hour - the man they had reviled only a little while ago! The man who was supposed to be against the interests of the country. The street-boys began fighting in the bar and he heard the sound of feet over the counter and the clink of bottles. He rolled over and really gave up before someone must have smashed something over his head.

Most of the customers tried to leave quickly. A few they got hold of and undressed, especially the man with the tie. They put it round his penis before they beat him with broken bottles and threw him out bleeding into the streets. Then they sat on the sheets in the rooms that the girls used to occupy. They found only one girl and they stripped her, put her over a bar-stool and took turns. She didn't seem to mind. One of the soldiers left his gun and joined in. Another one wanted to shove his rifle-butt up the girl's bottom, but some others prevented him. Two or three men fought in the lavatory over a boy, and a dead man downstairs burst open at the seams and sent a stench upwards that still left the intruders as determined as they had come. One of the late-comers said,

"Na Grandman that one what the soldier kill?"

Nobody answered. Instead all he could hear was broken glass and flying voices and a woman groaning, partly in ecstasy, partly in love. Before he made his way up the stairs of the hotel, someone smashed the glass, disconnected the wiring and the word "Paradise" fell with a clatter on the street below.

Opposite an old man and his children prayed to Allah and in the next house Sunday had a dry dream because women came and went and the evening of youth was so long. Tomorrow, he thought, when I'm big.

*       *       *

When Dr. Pietro came to, he smelt the unmistakable smell of unrotting dead. Dead who had been thrown out into the same cemetery he had known for so long and who had peed and died again in deadland with memories of their fright. He could not raise himself up and the earth was an inch from his nose. There was no sky that he could see - was there ever a sky?

A rawboned lady next to him sat up and said, "Na long time now they kill

127

me. Two days. Soon I go rotten and so I no business dey." She laughed.

Her husband, or a man near her, pulled her back down. He said, "Eh? Even when you done die you no go left for talk?"

She was soon talking again, "Na so 'e for be - you no 'gree?" she asked herself.

A small-boned white-moustached man took his hand off his penis and began crying.

The woman said, "When me own time, when I no been die, I been for make you happy. Na so I do when I been get life. I comforted. Always. Now I can happy you, like how I make the soldier and the street-fighter. He want give me his rifle-butt." She laughed again.

The man near her fell asleep again and the man with the white moustache began clawing an irregular way across the dust near her.

"Come," she called, "in this dirty we can make life alive. You get pickin?"

The man shook his head. "I believe that I'm a virgin but I've forgotten; it's such a long time ago. One forgets."

"A virgin?" she laughed and opened her legs.

The man who was sleeping next to her woke up and hit her with what looked to Dr. Pietro like a coffin-lid. "You no lay down?"

She said nothing and she lay still until the other figure had found his way over the grave-mounds and the unsightly bodies of the unburied dead.

"You won't laugh at me?" he asked.

She placed her fingers on her lips. Her thigh skin was shrunken almost to nothing and one breast had been left somewhere else. The man began an uncomfortable, ugly movement on her and Dr. Pietro felt like someone peering through a lavatory door.

"You no know for put 'am in?" she whispered.

The man cried again and rolled off, his eyes closed. He twitched twice and somehow, automatically, his finger went back to his penis and he lay still. Dr. Pietro saw the long corridor ahead of him; he felt like stumbling but he walked on.

"Dele?" he screamed. "Dele?"

*     *     *

After the crying and the walking along the deserted streets and the soldiers against the wall when she had come, wet like a towel and someone

128

had kissed her, tongue out and she had fought just a little, they had ground her and loved her into the dust. One man (in the dark she could never find him again), had a penis that pointed upwards almost towards his navel and when he had jammed at her she had felt the crown of his very point jabbing at her like a sword-fish. It was like the sweetness of first love.

Another time she had liked it; three men were making love to her. One was pawing her, another stood over her in his barefeet, his toe right up her and a third had beat and kissed her. They were so silent though, almost as if they were executing some strange ritual of living. From somewhere a dog had appeared and licked her breasts to power, and then her waist had started moving and the man had slapped her vigorously with the love and the yearning of those who are born strong. She had sat up and licked someone. She wondered afterwards whom; when they had finished they had left her lying there.

It was strange that the sun still rose and the sky was still crimson and blue. Strange that in spite of it all, this new dying had woken no soul in her. After this no man could give her love, not Sir Ianty, not Dr. Pietro, not Grandman. Perhaps only the dead could love her with a still penis and cold lips and thighs that neither moved nor gave way.

Her belly was a bag, that had held the semen of every male man who had come straight to her womb. Even a woman once, she thought. She had loved her during one rainy season and in the wooden house where she lived with her grandmother, she had explored her. Thelma's hands were sweet, much gentler than a man's. Thelma's love was soft on her lips, so soft that the kiss was one of love not desire. Thelma's fingers up her were like the soldier-boy's toes. Thelma had gone and left her in a grown-up world with men. Men were always lovers and adversaries, never friends.

"Dele? Dele?" She heard the cry and turned over on the ground. For the first time she realized that blood was oozing from her nose. She licked it and fell asleep thinking of Thelma's periods.

"Dele? Dele?" She did not move. It was sweet to sleep the sleep of those who had been given a new lease of death. Why this crier from another town? There had always been paradise. There had been no expulsion, until now. Sex was sweet in the morning and before tea. And love in the afternoon near the sea was even more beautiful and everlasting. Death was a recognition of all life. That those who bathe near the sea and the dark rocks that cultivate sea-snakes are those who truly die when the sea pulls them down in quicksand. No obituaries. No bones left to drape cemeteries.

"Dele? Dele? Where are you?" That unnatural voice.

129

She thought: Here where they had left me and my left leg slightly up against a wall because I was always wanting, and my right touching the ground because I was always giving out of my bowels the kind of need that the earth knows of a man's hunger. Here near the in and out of foam and salt-water. Soon the sea would take me like Grandman in its arms and I would come once, twice in the knowing that this was love. Love that passes. That's all. It can be understood? In this lightness near water and beachsand. In this movement of froth now caressing my brow with the tingle of mortal man, with the gentle fingers of Thelma.

Blood did not matter. It was what we all were. If it came out it reminded us of ourselves. That's why the menstrual cycle was so important; it was a reminder. And the blood on the streets, near shop-walls, on cobble-stones, the blood from slaughter houses, the blood that all this had brought on itself was the reminder that life was everlasting and death always imminent when she pointed her toes sky-wards and a man, any man, had gone round and round her navel spinning and panting. The saltwater touched her lips and someone lifted her, gently. Perhaps Thelma had come back with her papertowels and her hands like butter. Perhaps they would come together in the sea and caress the curl of wave on the mattress of blue. She could forsake herself, now a woman, wholly and completely, as she had done when a girl.

*     *     *

Sunday awoke with a pain in his belly. It was still half-dark. He saw his mother standing over him.

"Don't worry! They won't have you," she consoled him. She began to tell him a story about how the first women were made, how a man was climbing a tree with an axe and the axe fell and wounded his friend. The man then climbed down and tried to sew up his friend's wound with his penis.

"My wound is bleeding," she said to Sunday. "Now I can talk to you - you're a big boy, aren't you. It's tomorrow."

The boy held his stomach and vomited over the side of the bed, cream with a slight trace of blood.

"You'll be all right, I know. You'll be okay, for certain. God lives upstairs." Sunday tried to raise himself up a little. "Last night - " he began weakly.

"Yes you had a wet dream. It is because of the season. The dry season will come. Then rain does not flow then. I know. There is much that I know."

"But Mummy who is my father?"

She sat down abruptly on the side of the bed, her head pointing in the distance.

"Did I not tell you before? Eh? Did I not tell you?"

He sank back down and she looked at the stain that his youth had made when anxious women came and wept in his dreams at night. He was exhausted and sick.

"You have got to get better - try hard!" She breathed heavily and searched frantically about the room as if for someone.

*    *    *

It was the same house in which she had grown up. Cousin Cordelia had married and moved. Her grandmother was buried in the white-capped cemetery at Regent. Stephan had come perhaps twice and then he had gone. Nothing was left. The morning would come back here though and the night would go away to another place. She had naked herself to Cousin Cordelia the day she came and said about Stephan. It was famble business - why did Cousin Cordelia have to bellow from the streets, pulling hints the way she always did?

"Me," Cousin Cordelia had snorted. "Eh me?" She thumped her breast violently. "You no know say me be Mrs." No one answered her. Dele's grandmother was out and the sleeping pickin mostly off to school. Cousin Cordelia addressed the Foulah man's stall and a packet of leftover cigarettes. "To God! Na shame meet me this day," she insisted to a deaf-and-dumb tin of sardines. "Na shame thing I hear. Lawd have mercy!"

The Foulah man said, "I uncomprehendingly go give you for cheap. These days dem dear. I go give you for cheap."

"He is cheap. They get am cheap. Na nasty bitch! No get shame! Call down disgrace on me 'ouse."

Then Dele had joined in, at first only petulantly, from the window. "'Ouse? You get 'ouse? Which 'ouse you get? All your mortal days no you momma 'ouse you did leave in? Which time, excuse me, you purchase 'ouse?"

"Na disgrace you want disgrace me?" Cousin Cordelia asked a small crowd that was beginning to form. "I get shame and I get respect. No person here go disrespect me."

Dele opened the window wide and violently pushed at the wooden shutters that at first refused to give way.

"Me no get nothing to shame," she jumped on a table and yelled.

"Nothing!" She paused for breath. "Me not the first person pregnant with bastard. God go help me!"

"God and your front side - is like spring." Cousin Cordelia laughed loud and raucously. The crown joined in.

It was then that Dele made for the door. From next door the old pa began chuckling. The crowd increased. A few put down their loads; others stood near their cycles. At least one motorist stopped. This was a palaver and always made good hearing.

"I will samman you - you hear - I will samman you. You molest me character."

"Your character dey in front, under your dress," Cousin Cordelia rejoined. The crowd laughed and Dele was by then at the bottom of the four steps and over the zinc gate. She threw it open.

"Yes I get something under me clothes. Look am!" She ripped her clothes off and tugged at her brassiere. An American took a photograph. Two cyclists decided that it was more interesting to continue their journey. One palaver was like another. The man with the suit and the tie who had come from the car peered with increasing interest from the back of the crowd.

"Look me, look you - who want you? Look me, look you. Me own thing sweet past you. Na that make you dey jealous me. You bring *koko* to me. Na kill you want kill me," Dele bellowed.

"Look am," an elderly lady said, unknown to either. "Look am! E no get shame."

"Shame my backside! Youself - who call you? Na me and me aunty make small table-talk. What thing do you left here? Dele inquired.

The woman turned her back, made a sucking noise of disgust and one of the cyclists came back. A woman began doing a thriving trade in roast meat.

One of the munchers grunted, "You hit 'am Aunty. You fo' show am."

Dele stood, legs apart, hands akimbo. "If she is called woman, let her come. I will razor her rass." She spat once, twice and then again in the gutter. A small boy was trying his best, meantime, to make for a pot of rice, someone in the crowd went "hss" and he drew back suddenly, pretending that he was picking up one of the dress-cloths that had been put out to dry in the washyard.

Dele, meanwhile, threw herself on the ground, face downwards. "Bastard witch!" she screamed. "Come kill me! Come kill me."

By then Cousin Cordelia was roundly upbraiding the woman who had intervened. She was screaming, "People in these country no get respect you hearee? For what thing do you come? Notta me and me sister pickin make small palaber?''

The woman turned round and was about to reply when Dele decided, "He get right fo' talk. This stranger decent woman pass you. Na me see 'am with a man doin' the thing. Me own uncle na shame make 'e die. All the time na hypocrite you did play.''

Then the intermediaries intervened with "You no fo' worry - you aunty no get sense" to her, and to her aunt, "Na small stupid pickin." Dele branded them all as blasted hypocrites who could go to hell - you hear - go to hell - but she allowed them to pull her back into the house. That was the first time Sunday had kicked as if to say she had done well by him.

"Blast you all! Get out!" she had bellowed. She was a proud woman and Sunday was going to be the new generation. Which one of those cock-swingers could deserve him? Dr. Pietro, Sir Ianty or Grandman with his stupid visions?

And this was why she could not answer the boy. She had wondered herself when she woke near the sea, near the rocks in a morning that drizzled with small light rain. The foam was the sea spitting and the horizon was a dish of water in her hand. I love this boy who has left his youth behind for his age to come down on him like people's hands in a palaver.

*   *   *

Grandman had knocked late on the same zinc gate that he remembered. The streets were almost empty. In the distance, along the main road the night-drivers passed restlessly up and down.

"Dele? Dele?"

No answer. She used to sleep in a room just at the back and she would hardly hear him. But that was a long time ago. It was rather late but he had to see her. Decisions had to be made. Tomorrow he would be big and he was not at all sure. Suddenly he turned round and he saw her standing behind him.

"It's curfew time," he said by way of admonition.

"Still the old protector," she replied.

Then she opened the gate and he went into the yard that he had known so well. The coal-pot had gone out; mortar and pestle stood in the corner. She led him up the stairs. Like a blind man he followed her. Not far away he could hear the rum-and-coffee cries of mourners at a waking. Do the dead survive?

133

# CHAPTER 10

Sir Ianty remembered the time that Stephan's grandfather died. He was usually a healthy person but one day he got very ill. Almost before they could get the doctor, two pious gentlemen arrived requesting to see his wife. They were dressed completely in black from head to foot and after introducing themselves, said to her "We are very sorry to hear about Grandfather's illness."

His mother nodded, a tear in her eye.

"We have come to sympathize and to offer our services," the gentlemen intoned.

Their services proved both elaborate and expensive, for they were the local undertakers and they traced out the dying like vultures. Every day they must have drawn up a list, then eagerly gone from one address to the other, scenting out the dead. Sir Ianty often wondered how people became undertakers. Does some little gloomy six-year old turn to his father and say, "You pretend to be dead. I want to be an undertaker when I grow up"?

These undertakers offered the sorrowing mother before Stephan's grandfather was even properly dead, the following services:

(a) Luxury funeral - $2400 - The coffin was made of a special insect-proof wood and the corpse was to recline on satin cushions. There was to be a sliding panel of glass and special vases for flowers. It was however to be regretted that the brass handles supplied with the coffin had to be returned after the service.

(b) Middle-type funeral - $1200 - Sometimes called "Tourist Class to Paradise." The coffin in this case would be quickly diminished by insects. The sliding panel was made of wood not glass, but glass would be provided and the cost was $150. For another $20 the brass handles could be loaned.

In addition there were all sorts of accessories provided. If you opted for

(a) and paid a little more, then a longer oration was made for the dead person. If you opted for (b) then everything was hurried through as two (b's) made an (a), and the undertaker's point was to bury as many as possible as quickly as possible.

Another extra provided was hired mourners. They would break out into loud crying for as long as they were paid. Twenty minutes of uninterrupted wailing could cost as little as ten dollars. For less than five dollars, you had to do most of the crying yourself.

This used to take place a long time ago for in Iota death was a very delicate and finely worked out business. You could die if you wanted but never in peace. Even after the funeral, relatives were forced to insert doggerel verse in the Sunday papers, and wives who hated their husbands were compelled to write:

> 'Tis one year since you left me
> To go beyond the skies
> You left me only memory.
> And a heart that cries and cries.

Sir Ianty used to wonder who wrote the verses and what rhyming dictionaries they used and who paid them - until he found out about the Rev. Two-for-Three.

When he went to America soon after Stephan, he was surprised to learn that Americans treat death like a hot dog - something that is soon over and done with. He never saw undertakers pestering the relatives of the deceased. He never saw long columns in the Sunday papers proclaiming the virtues of the deceased. Equally he had never seen such a casual attitude to death. He had been accustomed to long processions of cars, trucks, bicycles and a hearse. Instead a funeral in San Francisco was two taxis and a dead man urgently attempting to make for the cemetery before rush-hour.

The most difficult thing about burying people in Iota at that time was that you were not allowed to die on a Thursday night. He remembered that this was carefully explained to him by a well-meaning official. The offices that deal with these matters were not open on Friday; so, he was advised, sick people must be kept alive until either Friday evening or should be encouraged to expire on Wednesday night, but never on Thursday. He once tried to get someone buried on a Friday and for one day he was the local undertaker in Iota before independence.

136

The first problem was where. An earnest Englishman from the Health Department (Why did the Health Department deal with death?) asked Ianty, "But this chap who is dead - is he Junior Service or Senior Service?"

Ianty didn't know.

"He drives a Volkswagen," Stephan had said helpfully.

The official stared at them.

"And he has morning tea," Ianty had ended, suddenly remembering.

"Ah!" was the reply. "Well that sounds like Senior Service."

"Why do you ask?" Stephan demanded, always wanting to start an argument.

They had visions of people on their way to the great beyond being lined up into two divisions, Senior and Junior Service, each man in his proper station.

"Oh it's about the burial," the official replied, "We have separate burial grounds for Senior and Junior Service."

Which was a neat way of saying for the English and the others. The matter was settled quickly, for even though people were not allowed to be buried on Friday, they understood that an exception had to be made in the case of Senior Service people.

The next problem was to find a hole. The Health Department would allocate a spot but Stephan and Ianty would have to find people to dig it. They agreed to do this and at the cemetery collected four earnest, sad-faced gravediggers who looked as if they had just come out of Hamlet. They assured them of their expertise and the two boys left them to it. The surprise came in the evening, when the minister's last words had sounded across the quiet cemetery: "Dust to dust, ashes to ashes." This was the signal to lower the coffin. But when they tried, it refused to go. The hole was too small. The gravediggers explained that they thought it was for a Senior Service child. A woman wept saying, "He doesn't want to go."

Needless to say all this has been changed. In modern Iota there are now undertakers (proper ones) and Sir Ianty himself had airconditioned his intended restingplace. Matters have much improved. The living can look forward to death and can indeed die any day and do.

*     *     *

Sunday saw all with the eyes of a child and heard with the ears of the innocent, born wise. Chen, chen, choo; chen, chen, chen; no mind can climb it, the children had shouted as they riddled in chorus. At first he did know and

137

then he realized that it was this smoke, the small mist outside that ran to him out of the world that was silent except for the single hook and small eye of a ferry. In fact the wake had ended for those who had fallen amongst the rocks and Grandfather had laughed. It was Whole Monday at Easter.

Again those voices which sought to give him no redemption but a second chance at having a new dialogue with worlds he had forgotten. The chorus behind his head chanted:

> *Every neighbor is my brother, is my sister.*
> *A moon follows us wherever we go.*
> *Hear oh hear!*
> *Sea is deep like a big man.*
> *Every brother, every sister is my neighbor.*
> *And this world is round and small.*

Hear oh hear! He heard the shout of women from the Bundu home where the initiation took place, "Hi jo! Hi jo!" screaming of small girls mingled with the ritual sound of the clitoris being cut. At burial time they would lead this same girl, now a grown woman, to the waterside at sundown. But before this final washing the girl with the tiny breasts would be bathed and would see herself in front of a mirror. The boys, fresh from their own initiation in blood, the beating of the turtle shell and the burial in the hole, would sing like them at sunset. If only those voices could remember all of the secrets of the bush! Then the masked leader spoke through painted lips that made her sound arresting and frightening.

1st Voice:    You ask me to remember
(Dele)        When remembering is best forgotten.
           I remember once the smell of raw wood
           Off Krootown Road. I remember the nails -
           He used them to make chairs and crosses.
           Even once he made a coffin for my grandmother . . .

           You ask me to remember that day
           I was all alone or was I?
           It is so hard remembering
           When remembering is best forgotten . . .

O those lights under my feet at Wilberforce
And the *bobos*, hardly *bobos*, outside the hotel
"Make I was' de car . . ."
It was a long walk up Pademba Road to Cotton Tree!
I remember so much and so little.
Dry season end and rain just begin to tumble
And the tourists had come to peer through binoculars . . .

2nd Voice:    O my child, you cannot know it all,
(Grandman)  For knowing is the death I feel.
               The itch in the ribs,
               The small, tall pain that begins in the bowels
               And the knowledge that you are the last old man.

1st Voice:     But I remember (*laughs*) I remember.
(Dele)         Remembering is not best forgotten
               I was small, barefoot, only a *pickin*.
               The kap kap kap of *titi* footwear
               Was still unworn. Then in country cloth
               I ran behind the man - how tall he was!
               The crowd was dancing in the streets
               And for no reason I danced with them.
               That woman, the mad cripple, spat at him,
               But the man walked - ten feet high.
               I thought: if I were only three feet high
               I would bury myself at sundown - *Hi jo*!
               Women would dance over my grave and tie their heads.

2nd Voice:    No madman wants children to pass on his left side.
(Grandman)  I will sell sasswood to Susu.
               That was no *awoko* man; at Christ Church the bell rang once.
               Obituary for schoolchildren.

1st Voice:     Hush for cut heart! I heard the little voices
(Dele)         Of men who were hungry but did not know his thirst.
                When the witchbird comes at night after
               The zinc gate has been padlocked, it's *koko*.

Only cassava leaf and pans beaten with a cry:
    Ko-ko-go
    Ko-ko-go
    Ko-ko-go
Can stop that bird from crying.

2nd Voice:   Did the bird cry? Did the bird cry?
(Grandman) At sundown I heard the voice of a rooster.
           The first betrayal of those who knew him well.
           For thirteen pieces of copper.
           It was better the picking was
           A stoop-down than a stand-up.
           It was better those three
           Did not shout "Ah give you joy"
           After the hotels had refused them and they
           Had walked the town at sunfall
           Until stable-time.

1st Voice:   Pa, you speak in riddles, pulling hints.
(Dele)       You say remembering is best forgotten.
           But I remember *ronshoo* and his morning feet
           His bag, his gun.
           I remember one foot jumbie and the
           Thump of his footsteps at night
           (*Laughs*) I had always wanted a doll-baby
           Will you give me a doll-baby?
           I will not sweep dust at night
           I will eat one-pot rice when the time is no longer soft.

2nd Voice:   He was a hot man and when that woman
(Grandman) Outside the hotel washed his feet in the gutter
           The boys laughed - kya, kya - but it was morning
           And the singing beggar-woman touched him.
           She who had never seen washyard nor flush-latrine
           Charcoal or salt for cleaning teeth . . .
           You are not the soil of this place,
           One woman said. I wondered what she meant then
           Until Grandman grew from Stephan.

| 1st Voice: | Hush ya, hush for buryin' |
| (Dele) | Raincoat judge could find nothing wrong with this man. |
| | I wanted to take my cloth - red and white - to the fetish man. |
| | On Wednesday when I married they should all say |
| | You done do good, but no one spoke. |

Later they will use Bible and ring
In the name of, in the name of . . .
What names they call? He had liked
Foo-foo and bitter leaf, krin-krin, sour-sour,
Beans and palm oil, especially ginger-beer and rice bread.
At the end he wanted only dying
So everything could be tidier in the streets.

| 2nd Voice: | (*Loudly*) No! A man does not stumble and fail |
| (Grandman) | At harvest-time near a cotton-tree. |
| | Then is the ripening when leaves are clean. |
| | But he saw the green mangoes in their fullness |
| | And he knew their fall-time |
| | When the seed divorces the branch - |

| 1st Voice: | And the schoolgirls, out of uniform, |
| (Dele) | Begin their corner-corner |
| | I was one of them and I saw him |
| | Just beyond the glass-pale of his car |
| | And he was weeping. |

He was full, he said, and yet there was
An empty ache in his bowels,
A fever in his brain.
He had not loved enough,
Built only one citadel near Signal Hill.
And the house he had fashioned,
Was like a skeleton which others do not know.
I remember, although remembering is best forgotten,
He lay flat on his bowels and died.
Why are the dead so selfish?
And now not a one to remember him.
The dead are so selfish.

There was of course the ceremony,
Wakes are for the living
For Grandman lay with the uncomfortable dead
And the ache in his bowels had gone.

2nd Voice:    But the earth -
(Grandman)

1st Voice:    Yes my brother, the earth does not grow fat.
(Dele)        The Grandfather had said so.
              The panel lights go off and on.
              There is a dent at the very rear of the earth
              And no woman knows her own face in the mirror . . .
                    *mi mami bin dey telkl me sey*
                    *tranga yeys noh gud.*
                    *a noh yeri,*
                    *tranga yeys noh gud.*

2nd Voice:    (*Firmly*) But he did not die.
(Grandman)    That we can be reasonably certain of
              When the purple hills are like a package
              Which the sky has wrapped up and
              The faded brown trees climb down seawards -

1st Voice:    But I saw it, child as I was.
(Dele)        The sea was big water that day
              When they pulled him off Cotton Tree
              And left him near Lumley Beach
              And the night came and went with the surf-bathers.

2nd Voice:    (*Almost to himself*)
(Grandman)    I remember when the world was green before the ripening
              The palm-trees that walked to the edge of Number Two Beach
              And three handfuls of rice on the feast of Greater Beiram.
              Songs of women from the Bundu Bush.
              All time, everywhere.
              I had never thought of myself as going to my own funeral.
              I who was neither old nor young

142

Who saw the chatterbox weaverbird
And the parable of a woman, no longer girl,
After the chants and chorus in the Bundu home.

Remembering, my dear, is best forgotten.
What can I tell you about the agony in Victoria Park?
Of the soldiers who took him away?
It is not easy to begin at the beginning
For is it the forest out of which we hack our way at night?
Or the morning on the Taia River
And the ferry-boats that take us near cataracts?

1st Voice:    Pa, I beg, don't pull your rusty proverbs.
(Dele)       You are old with dust.
           You have gone too often up and down Westmoreland Street
           Looking for Bai Bureh's shadow.
           Tell me how it happened.
           Between the impatient hoot of Grandfather's ferry-boat
           And that long last journey to Cotton Tree
           When the boys came out to laugh.

2nd Voice:    The truth is that I don't remember all.
(Grandman) I cannot be sure how much of what I say is true.
           There were plasticene men, a man with a torn jacket.
           A pair of crutches and, in somebody's backyard,
           A mango tree, stalk-bright, the color of sand.

           Grandfather sat in a rocking chair, high up.
           He hardly spoke.
           Large and black, he had the left fourth finger
           Of his right hand chopped off.
           I came at the tail-end of his love-time.
           I am sure that you remember - you could not
           Possibly forget such a casual act.
           We commit a hundred every day riding blindwards
           Between the jungle and the cataracts.

| | |
|---|---|
| 1st Voice:<br>(Dele) | Is it of LOVE you speak?<br>The love that passeth - |
| 2nd Voice:<br>(Grandman) | No, child, the love that *is* understanding.<br>Do you remember the night when you followed the man.<br>You ran, clickety-clack, on the points of heels<br>Little holes in the soil<br>Stiff road pressing against the tip-tap<br>Of calf-leather and steel-point.<br>A watchman heard you and turned over in his dreams<br>The booze singing in him.<br>And Sunday heard and dreamt a dream - |
| 1st Voice:<br>(Dele) | (*Loudly in anger*)<br>But how can you know, old fool, how can you know? |
| 2nd Voice:<br>(Grandman) | (*Rising*)<br>And this was the evening of the first day<br>And Grandman, proud man, walked the streets.<br>It was near-night and in this my city<br>Which had never loved me,<br>But which in spite of everything I had always worshipped,<br>I saw shimmering light and leaf-fringe.<br>Now, at this very hour, children in the dry up-country<br>Would be reciting Muslim *suras*.<br>I walked past the houses where the gentry lived<br>And at Signal Hill, I could look down on this,<br>My city, and adore the testament of twinkling lights.<br>All round the sea coveted the land.<br>No church then, high on every village hill,<br>Waiting for a Sunday waking. |
| 1st Voice:<br>(Dele) | (*As from a distance*)<br>Now I see your face, those features<br>At one with agony and mirth.<br>Those hands criss-crossed<br>Bore life aloft.<br>I remember what I do not remember. |

144

The cyclists laughed and yet you went your way.
A policeman in Saunders Street lay down.
They led two beggars out with you.
I remember what I do not remember,
For remembering is not best forgotten.

All this was in the eyes of the child who had been circumcised with sorrow and who had mated the hurt and denial of his grandfathers. In his eyes too the sorry coming and the wisp of familiar moon that had followed Yacub and the slaves. All night the slaves had sung like towers. From where they lay, packed body on body, they had mated in their first fast night before the White sailors had flogged the more potent, coming where the sea goes and the moon cannot follow. And all came to a turning point that generations later would not be able to unturn.

From the plantations they had taken the life of the land at twilight when they sang snatches of something they could barely remember. They threw this new agony like a *buba* over their shoulders. I was a burden but never a belonging and beneath the half-flimsy cloth that concealed one man from his neighbor, still lay a soul - twisted, shining, but smooth. It was the rock-kind out of which they would later carve their churches in a different haven and a strange earth.

On the plantations, long before the Brown Party, long before the Fair Party, long before the imposition of a foreign will, everything was dead. Except by the river the illusion of life persisted. Darkness was a long spear and it pierced morning into a new wonderness. There was something there, the boy thought, formed and yet formless. Neither fog nor water for it would not go. And yet again those voices!

The boy saw the lower half of lips that moved, two or three closed eyes that were yet alive, a formless body with no face, shapeless masses in the room. The yellow presence of an unknown thing. The devil's mask looked at him. It had gone into jungle, into watering places and desert and he felt its wonder through a single heartbeat. Eyes that were at first light, grew dark. He remembered kicking the wind, blowing the songs and the forms away; he would understand, for his eyes were filled with tears. Dele asked him, "Why? Why? Why?"

There was the rustle of her dress as she came close to her son, and he smelt her old-world smell which was his breath and her breathing.

"You have no father. I had husbands. Three - Stephan, the beautiful boy

145

who was later Grandman. Then Ianty, and after him Pietro."

"It doesn't matter," the boy replied. "Husbands are for loving. Children for life." He was surprised at what he had said.

"All finished me," she continued.

He could hear the venetian blinds rattling again. And suddenly it was morning. The voices went, except for one that kept haunting him: "Men walk with heavy shoes; their hands are hard. You are young, a boy, my son. The love I bear you is in my breast and my bowels. Walk near me - the lights of the whole world are downstairs."

She reminded him of another land of kola but told him that now new men must start again. After the long procession and the mortar-board drumming which sounded out the rhythm meaning life, the dawn would open up like the women who came wet in his dreams. Of course there had been once upon a time, some time. In this new land, woods must burn bright, but without fire. For time had turned round. Forget the dry months, the cruel pain in the bowels, the first stab in the street and the shimmering points of soldier-boy's bayonets. These do not matter. We have met, loved and are now silent.

# CHAPTER 11

"I belonged," Dr. Pietro was saying, "to a generation that did not know the truth."

"Yes the truth," Grandman insisted, "was what I made it. I tell you," he got up and looked through the windows of Dr. Pietro's place. He could see the white-capped cemetery all round. He began again, "I tell you it matters about people - it never did before. Ianty was a complete ass! That was why I went to jail. That's why he's alive."

"Yes it does matter about people," came a soft rejoinder from Dr. Pietro.

For a moment there was silence in the room. Grandman walked over with some obvious agitation and tried Pietro's radio.

"Nothing - nothing yet."

"My profession," Dr. Pietro continued, "has told me something about people. That they matter in a strange way. My job was to prevent them from lying out there." He made a vague thrust with his head towards the cemetery.

Grandman did not reply. Then he said, "You didn't ask me why I came or who sent me and why to you?"

"Does it matter?" the other asked. "I suppose I'm right for anybody now. But I still believe that nothing is really good except that with which we can change the world."

"Change the world?" Grandman asked, "In Iota, this small place where the sea brings the garbage from all the world's corners, what change can there ever be?"

Dr. Pietro lit a cigarette and laughed a small harsh laugh. "You don't even believe in your own revolution then?"

"No," the other replied. "It is like larger revolutions. The good deeds of whores and pimps and a single boy who must grow up into a better world."

Dr. Pietro flicked ash carelessly into an ash-tray on a low whisky stool.

He said nothing but one had the feeling that he was listening more intently.

"The first woman was the first whore. Their children belong to us."

Dr. Pietro laughed again. "Your genetics seem slightly dated now. I thought only one of us could have him."

"Sunday is not our problem. Only insofar as we don't have to own him. We won't ever. I feel that it only matters about the quick trip he makes from pacifier to old man's chamber-pot. He has to be remodeled like the latest large passenger aircraft."

"I am sorry to come back to my profession. The intestines are the same. Blood is still red and the heart still stops beating. But I grant you one thing - he's alive and so is the cripple near the cemetery. Dele is like us. As a matter of fact the very Ianty that you despise is alive, because he is a clown like Two-for-Three. I don't feel particularly benevolently disposed towards them - not any of them."

Grandman did not reply directly; instead he said. "It's strange. I've never liked raw earth or flowers or coffin-wood. Yet your new room looks well."

The other nodded. "My own business was with the so-called living. I tied up their guts, chopped up their insides, scooped out tape-worms, healed fevers in the brain - and all the time my hands were full of blood. Not now, though. Thankfully I am left without the necessity for encounters or declarations. For the first time the whole world is reordered for me - I who had feared darkness, who struggled in the isolation in which I found myself in every love-encounter, now know that communication can take place between that proud, silent world of all that is inanimate and the me that I have become."

"They built a pyre and burnt a whole heap of us together. A barefoot man scraped us all together and dropped us somewhere. I don't know where. It's not important. Before I always used to wonder where they had buried my navel cord. I used to think about my grandfather - strong, Black, silent. Now even that does not matter."

"Yes," Dr. Pietro agreed. "There is no longer the infinite loneliness. There is companionship in dust." He put out his cigarette. "I had spent so much time trying to prevent the unspoken communication with the silent. That was a good doctor's work."

"And I," Grandman added, "so much in attempting to preserve our efforts of order. I felt that was the job of a politician - or dictator if you like. But there is an order amongst these white tombstones. The difficulty is to transmit that to the living. How can they see, hear and understand? How can they be told they have set up a punitive force in authority over them, that their very

148

selves are numb with fear of the soul? That there is no way away from the authority of public destruction?"

"Well there is no going back. There might be ways of letting the others know. I shall write Sunday. I might even call it a novel. Sunday will read it. I shall tell him that the world is imponderable. That he should begin instead to think about the smaller things that do not matter, as he sees it - cockcrow, the first laughter from the chatterbox weaverbird."

"We cannot be put out like a light. Not that we are shadows. We will arrive tomorrow and tell them about the agues we have felt in the tomb. We are witnesses of the catastrophe that beckons every mortal man from secret corners. If only we arrive, they can no longer doubt."

"You are just the same bossy old-fashioned dictator. Have you asked me about the journey? Do you know if I wish to go or not? I said I would write a letter. I said I would tell them how to disentangle themselves from pettiness and the serfdom of daily bread. But to return - no! To be driven away from herding with coconut trees back to that wound which was life! To undergo that ache again! Thank you, Grandman! You shall be the missionary! It's too early for me to spend my own death!"

Dele stirred between them. She spoke to herself, "I have lost all. My misery, my apathy." She sat up, eyes staring straight ahead. "Tell me what sex I am."

Dr. Pietro said to her. "You helped me murder myself. I had to do this if the spirit in me was ever to be fulfilled. You are no longer whore or murderer. You are nothing."

"If I went out to them," Grandman mused, "and I told them that power was illusory, that they lived with unliving selves and had not attained the purity of corpses pitchforked under rubbish . . ."

"They would not understand," Dr. Pietro interrupted dryly. "Tell them that they must shatter the madness of their world; greatness is at an end and that the cripple with empty fingers clawing the dust is richer. Tell them to come with you; dawn rises from their rubbish-heap lives. There are no stars now. Their world has passed."

"Has sex passed too?" Dele asked sleepily. "What are the sacred duties that men can perform with women?"

The others looked at her. She continued. "None there will recall anything except red blood on the pavements. The soldiers shot because they did not want to mutiny."

The transistor crackled to life and a voice said words like "atrocities," "old order", "new laws", "ban the opposition".

Grandman said, "Now I know that all this has happened and those who tell did not experience it, and those who experience know that it needs no telling."

"What does it matter?" Dr. Pietro asked. He lay down. "I'm tired. Those voices I hear now shouting for peace are the very ones who sat at the foot of the king. At least thank heaven he's not here. It's bad enough having you Grandman, but Ianty would kill me!"

"Is this a time for jokes?" Grandman asked. "God, tomorrow is here and nobody knows how to stop fighting their fathers! It would be better if they understood the ritual burying of the navel cord. It would be better if they all thronged the oceans of the new world like Columbus to the healing place. The old world is dying, not our death, but a death that despairs of death."

"You speak of miracles," Dele said, "only love can engender the dissolution of the morally unstable and resuscitate from oblivion the voices of millions who have been made dumb. The guilt belongs to us. I for one have inflicted on an orphan the tragedy of procreation."

"Not you alone, Dele," Grandman replied softly. "The night they killed me so suddenly I had walked to Regent and I thought of the samelessness of all our guilts. Roof and windows, windows and roof. Let them fall, I thought. But I did not know that I would see all this terrible sameness. People in a million tombs, unlike ours, suffering from the same sickness."

"Tomorrow - ," Dr. Pietro began.

"Tomorrow is now," Dele shouted. "They must know the message, what we have learnt. We goats and sheep who have never sheltered under the same cellar, fraternizing in the mud. They must be told about man and woman and being together and the sanctuary of children."

"We have questioned long and wondered for many hours and what answers can we give since we are only playing with mortal destinies?" Grandman spoke softly.

"Life and death become one - no longer can your scalpel separate it, Pietro. One can be sure of nothing, neither the one that strides ahead nor you who come up to meet him. The wise man is he who knows that life is laughter."

"And laughter is half-agony, half-humor," Dele added. "If they can grin they can live. Destroy the illusions and feel the tender moments of their lives. Sex is nearly all. I gave you love and happiness for moments, didn't I?" she asked Dr. Pietro. "There is the meeting-hall where they can truly say, 'I give you joy' for every person has these words in him. But they must not be afraid, they must not for one moment doubt."

"Then we must all go back," Grandman said. "Pietro will show them that his surgeon's fingers can never arbitrate nor dare contrive to make division where none exists. You, Dele, will show them that their uncomfortable gyrations on four-posters is not a link but a cleavage with matter, and I - " here Grandman paused, "I will show them that calamitous though living is, there must be no capitulation to the disaster of revolutions."

\* \* \*

The venetian blinds that hung down from the roof of the board house moved slightly in the wind. Sunday sat up suddenly. He was a little better and then he tried to lie down again and to pull the blankets over him. He lay down in a liquid dark that seemed to move and throb with forms and the voices of those he had known, fathers of his who had left the world to him now. Now the cocks were fighting no more and the town was passive in God's palms.

He heard: "We have built the everlasting stone of the lost temples which you will find. Out of our madness and our shouting, out of our worry and the diseases of our brains, out of the scarred flower, a face, a new face, at once damned and sanctified, is forming."

\* \* \*

*Extract from Dr. Pietro's missive entitled "The Future of Tomorrow."*

... because of the flood and the fire, because of all the unwisdoms that have been uttered, because of the lack of form and order, there are a number of men who sleep without, women lying drunk or dead in gutters. All flights have been cancelled and living is postponed till the day after tomorrow. The blind tenants of the earth can no longer copulate because of their secret fear of guilt and the indecent lives of any two neighboring houses have the dull, bland look of the damned.

For the moment we have had to expel divinity as useless. The prayers we offered were not heard and those we did not offer stifled our breasts and kept us awake at nights fretting for a boy-priest who had died and whose wish it was to offer the last sacrament of ashes. He was so young - much too young for dying and when he fell cross-wise off his motorcycle, his catechism spurting blood, we could not think. The moment of forgiveness staggered and collapsed.

151

Those who are not sleeping are awake and drunk. Those who are not sick are lying in houses where walls have been blown away and private lives stare at the front garden. If one writes so much it might be misconstrued by the censors of the public ear. This is in fact what is to be expected at this time of the season; grass has been burnt dry but no new sprouts come up, and hungry cattle roam over deserts of parched earth.

One must get used to the piracy of the soul, for in the absence of sky-rockets, herbs keep company and there are no moon-men who can take us nearer oblivion, the slow progress from the rocking horse to the hearse. Perhaps not so slow since now that leaves are mildew and the afternoon air has been hung up to dry, short days crawl bedwards and street-lamps lift their faces sky-wards, to a moonless zone of which I cannot speak. Another winter is happening . . .

What then can I tell you? Death is not there in the sad afternoon, among the railings; it is not at another place standing and weaving patterns of light and darkness. It is in the warm scent of the rose, the shout of boys in the sand over the silence of damp, in the toss of hair-curl as a woman moves from charity to slumberless vanity, from grace to glory.

No sermon this but instead a narrative of the wreath's urgent need to the devotion of living. We will bury our dead when all living things have passed away from us. But only then. Only a second ago the children and the priest had laughed in the garden, and now in the latrine there is the crying of old men, spermless but speechful, knowing that they had done their own undoing and that the death that faced them was the death of glands, organs, speech and minor defects of the brain . . .

No doubt therefore it was all very sudden and perhaps it was the sadness more than the error which surprised us. Ordering was easy. We had of course made wills and testaments, consulted oracles and been discouraged, given discourses, sometimes learned, on the need for arriving. We who had never sired anyone, were never sure of anywhere, knew we had to go and hoped to arrive in good shape, sitting preferably in a first class compartment, with the weather fine. Last year this time I was in another place and I had thought that the days would never criss-cross. But they did, and now this. What have we? (The girl yawned and wondered if the boy-priest trusted her. In fact she did not care whether she arrived or not. They kept on talking and never got there. Sin and forget, they both thought, in silence. It was a false silence.)

True enough we were not warned of the demolition. Even the boy-priest who crashed, helmet and catechism in the dust, seemed unaware. Perhaps the poets knew or the girls near the well. One day we left home and came back to find unfamiliar spaces between the furniture. The room had turned completely round. When we spoke up, even air was no longer tidy, but there was of course still us - people called us by names we remembered and so we continued with the association we had with our members, forgetting for a while that we had become slightly hostile neighbors to ourselves. Even our vacancy was absent and the paradise-birds sang no more in tamarind trees. Our silences had gone.

Within this nightmare from which we did not wake, we waited. Some, pagan-like, for the worship of our true idols, others for the false gods of our cunning. No mind to watch with, no light in the bell-tower nor life in the belly. We waited. Nuns were lured into gardens of scent and shown pineapples which they bought. At some stage we must have realized in the dream that truth could never decide for us. Either we accomplish it or we dole it out to pawnbrokers . . .

My duty, my humility, my service, I thought. In times that were "historical," when we stood on the loneliest fringe of the world, looking over the abyss for company, we realized that since things were happening and we had scientifically controlled excessive growth of thorns and briar-patches, we must be ready for the ritual sacrifice of sheep. Instead we built a fountain, adorned it with memoranda, cyclostyled copies of minutes that had passed into hours and the phallic symbol which we could no longer remember. "In the very kingdom of Heaven, there is a bath and all who enter therein wash pride and lust away. Verily I say this to you. Simeon forgot his headphones," the priest used to say. Therefore those who went out late serenading love found false gods mouthing their anger.

We kept feeling and ought not to have continued to feel. There could be no crime, for were not things happening? But the re-enactment of disaster, unfettered to the manacles of fertile re-growth, had meant that to save a state in which God had died, we had to destroy all apologists, versifiers, doctors, lame men, weak dogs, politicians, parasites, saints, farmers, prostitutes, betrayers, strange faces, in fact all protagonists of repentances we did not want. So we unknowingly suffered, fully believing that a sinless season was impossible.

As we moved or seemed to keep standing, the temples fell. I will say this: they toppled with grace, full of dignity. Theirs was not the hooligan collapse of zinc on concrete but the thin tender surrender of flower on earth, the drizzle of pollen sprinkled on majestic grass sod. Of course there were protests; exiles prowled in every direction and genius was extinguished by clever dicks. No one could give answers to questions you did not ask. Of course the students and others who could not understand were sorry, but so were the tsetse flies.

153

"A world of manna is bad, but that with scapegoats is even better," the boy-priest mumbled before he died.

Then we came to yesterday and the defeat. It is easy to understand, for living had become an endeavor of the impossible and men receded to narcissism. No more marriages took place and after a time we did not even consent to breathing. Contraceptives and airfresheners were necessary. Genesis had ended. You have to know that for us life was a mistake and the cruel definition of it was that sorrow employed life as a joy-stick. We surrendered to the robbery and the fiction.

We mated with our own kind. Rubbing and friction were easier than the burial of the male organ in the female's and the joyful clutch of ovaries. We had to die - not fully knowing why, except that we had removed the causes of our being. We had become mere appendages, a curious anachronism in an age of mechanical order. The paradox was complete when the machines moved us, but left the parking-meters. We genuflected to soap-suds over our stainless steel sinks and the condensed world in the television box.

Now again there is singing. Someone in the silence has come in and gone out; one with visions. My new condition is like a river during the dry-season, wet without water. There is no need for me to pretend any longer for I know my own needs and failings. I am like a weaver: I wish to love all - my neighbor, the cook next door, all laymen, the boy from the bakery, the impatient man rattling typewriter keys late at night and butterflies. This, indeed, is the will of all that I was denied in flesh. I need no disaster now. The boy-priest's death was mine.

The headphones are on again and I am in tune with an eternal murmur of flies on a drowsy afternoon. I have achieved wealth, conquered passions, liquidated designs, circumvented disappointment, towered over terror. In this new conscience I can equate this with that and, having clearly heard the Soundings of the eternal mammoth, can give voice to the society of the sun that sings silence for the emir's coming.

And so I send you my breathings and my memories, the mistakes of a hundred lives and the necessity for looking back. Behind the garage wall the owls hoot in their sleep, and talkative sheep mutter the language of grass-shoots. There need be no exposure, no expulsion. Only survive. Flesh is the will of the someone who moves lightly in and out with grace, singing with the true silence.

I remain . . .

# POSTLUDE

The day awoke with the cry of a child. In the light womb-like darkness of pre-dawn it shattered the house and like a shock its strains spread outwards from the bedroom of the watchful ancestors to the dormant still ears of the sleepers. In this womb of a house, suddenly bathwater flowed like the first waters, and as in a ritual the people moved to the hint of sunlight and the gift of morning.

"Mornin' Granma," the young ones intoned spreadeagled on the floor.

"God's morning, children," the Female Elder replied and gave her blessing.

From the once hollow house, came the sound of early words spoken against the backdrop of first morning, like a man turning with his tongue the sounds he would next make into language.

"Mornin' Granpa," the children chanted. And the Male Elder stirred and heard the voice at his feet.

The children rose and made their way out of the Elders' quarters to where their parents were. The Male Second Giver of Life lay against the wall, his mouth half open to the healing ray that pried its way through the slit. Above him came the cry again; it was a shaft of light, penetrating, burning, and ecstatic. Its urgency woke the Male Second Giver of Life and he opened his hands wide in the empty womb-like enclosure and spoke God's blessings on all children who greet their parents on bended knees.

"May day receive you," he heard his own voice say. And the children bent their naked bodies and kissed the earth on which their elders trod.

With them he went and slowly, like a man at ease within himself, he put his robe on while the naked children watered. He held their hands but one child he clutched next to his bosom as he too went down on knees and hands to sing of morning joy. The Female First Giver of Life smiled as if she heard their

155

voices in a dream, coming from some other time. She opened eyes, still blinded by the sudden half-light.

"The day is good!" she greeted them.

Again the voice of that insistent child broke out again, over their heads and eyes and ears. They heard it and rejoiced.

The Female First Giver of Life enjoined them, "May this day remain forever green in memory. This child - our child - has but a moment's time with us. We must make it ready for that time. But children don't forget that here and now is over there and then, is back there and beyond. Let's teach it that."

All four went out and opened up the door and the screaming child came out head first into its first new day and dawn was red like blood against the sky.

"There is the Third Force," the griots sang at sun-up. "Neither Male nor Female but the neutralizing force that makes this miracle of bone and flesh."

By then the outer courtyard was full of the voices of the celebrants who had risen early on that special day and, on their way to farm and market-day had come first to give their greetings to the new-born child.

"Today," a voice said, "is the only day he knows."

"Yes," another agreed, "life gives us only one such every lifetime and today is its."

"And ours too," spoke still another, "for we have to labor and today at close of market day will know - "

"That comes both now and later," the Female Elder said. "Reward is all today. This thing we planted knows and does not know its fruit till sun-down."

Again that cry but now a softer cry, no longer piercing, for already its head had found a way out of the dark to the light outside. The cry was joyful as if celebrating the birth of first light. They brought the infant out and held it high up. The rays of the early sun bathed it gently like running water warmed with fire.

Now the child, no longer crying, was as still as ears. A kind of peace had come over it; a kind of peace that was holy and whole. In the radiance of that child's first day, no one spoke for sometime. The voices were still, for then they knew the language of words, but had not yet learned the language of the spirit. Slowly, suddenly a tremor came over the still infant and its mother raised it sky high to the blessing of light.

Now dawn had come and from around the world, all woke up to cockcrow and the sound of cartwheels, the morning songs of animals and the clatter of field instruments. Already the first group had set out to the farms and another to the market place. Already the hearth had been lit and the pots were being scraped. The blacksmith stirred the embers of his fire and touched his anvil; today he would invent a gift for life. The home-builder touched the rough mixture of his outside walls. Today he too would make a boon for the living.

Yet the child slept, no longer nervous, but with the kind of pleasure smile on its face. Girl or boy child, no one yet knew, for it would grow into this. So the griots say and, as the men and women went to tend their farms and homes, a leaf, but slightly tarnished with the dust of soil, had burst out of a dung-heap. Timidly, almost apologetically, the leaf lay idle on its frail stem, sleeping, like the child into some future which was now.

"This is the road on which you must forever walk," the Namemaker ordered. "The door you must close but ever leave open to passing strangers. This is the food you must eat, the work you must do, the pot you shall bear on top your head. This is the road on which you must forever walk," the Namemaker ended.

And all the assembly sang the birth of life at first dawn. All prayed and thanked the good earth out of which the leaf had sprung and the child was made. All spoke, at first in whispers then later just a trifle louder, for it was an early time. Then the Wise Fool spoke.

"It's only early morning. This is a long hard day. After the Naming Ceremony at dawn we, like the sun, must make our way to noon. And then high up recount our deeds and through our visions, foretell our own dusks. For later, when evening comes, and men and women creep in from the cold to warm themselves near fires, they must know this only--that the way did not come and go with just a swan song. They must know that on this day, this very day, we began the world."

He danced and jumped as he spoke thus, as if to music. Everyone laughed saying, "Fool, we can't take you seriously. It's too early for a joke."

"But listen just a moment," the Wise Fool continued, "It's not just words for deaf ears. It's a language which I speak - a broken one but one with which I'll give you - "

Yet they laughed again. His words were drowned in raucous bellows.

"He's already drunk," someone shouted, "and it's scarcely sun-up. I wonder what he'll say by sun-down."

Again the merry laughter as people drifted off. The child lay sleeping still and the leaf still sleeping lay. Finally? The Third Giver of Life knew the child which, neither male nor female, lay still within the leaf and yet within the child. This was neither man nor woman, good nor bad, up nor down. This could not easily be understood, since it embraced not one or two but three and made it whole.

On this first day when humankind was young and the Wise Fool joked and the sun broke out of the hill of clouds and made the day, on this first day had come the secret of creation of which only the Third Giver of Life had full knowledge, but which the child and leaf could feel. It could be theirs to use, for if they only understood it well, they could make the whole world whole.

Darkness hides its secrets well for in the night of earth, under roofs and within the womb, the leaf and child have known the secret of the Third Giver. Would they recall this at noon? Only light would know. Would they remember this at sundown? Only space would know. Would they complete the sun's journey back to darkness and to light again? Only the vast inscrutable incomprehensible force of the Third Giver could envision how a new-born leaf and a fresh child are so alike as they await the coming and the gone.